ROAR AT THE UNIVERSE

ALSO BY DANITH MCPHERSON

Monarch of Lightning
Book One of the Lightning series

Through the Wall
Short fiction

ROAR AT THE UNIVERSE

TALES OF CRISIS AND SURVIVAL

DANITH

McPHERSON

Wayward Serpent

These stories are works of fiction. Names, characters, places, events, and dialogue are either the products of the author's imagination or used in a fictitious manner. Any resemblance to actual people, living or dead, or to actual events or dialogue is purely coincidence.

First edition, first printing, March 2019

ISBN 978-1-950506-00-2
Library of Congress Control Number 2019902536
10 9 87 6 5 4 3 2 1

Cover Art: Beneath the Surface of the Long Prairie River, photography by D. L. Clausen

Published by Wayward Serpent
Up to no good but means well

To all the wonderful geeks and nerds in my life.

You make things so much fun.

CONTENTS

Introduction

To the characters within these pages and to those who read their stories:

Stuff happens. Really bad stuff happens. It shifts you into crisis mode, that state where you find yourself forced to do the unexpected; where you have to make it up while you're right in the middle of it; where you pretend you have a plan so you feel like you're in control, even though, just below the surface, you know you're not.

Sometimes it happens to you. It sneaks up like a predator and pounces without warning. You barely see the beast until it has you in its jaws. Fleeing isn't possible. There's no safe place to go anyway. Fighting is the only option. There are many ways to fight. You have to find your own.

Sometimes you purposely take a breath and charge straight into the fray. You know it's dangerous, but you're compelled to do it because of who you are—or, more accurately, because of who you want to be. That image of yourself you carry around in your daydreams would never stand still while the fire advances unchecked. And so you must become the person you are in your mind. If you don't, you'll lose your soul.

Bad stuff. You can be surprised by it and react in self-defense, or you can aggressively slam your fist into its gut. Either way, you roar in a desperate attempt to shatter an intolerable situation. You use whatever bits and scraps you can grasp to keep your tilting reality from collapsing like a toothpick landscape.

Don't expect the universe to be impressed by your efforts. Just know that you place your mark on the cosmos, even if it's only fingernail scratches through faded paint.

Folds of Blue Silk

This guy's chatting at me like an ancient Western. Red and black in the bar's moody lighting instead of colorized. Sophistication painted over frontier attitude. My fingerprints push shadows across the table so I won't look for the robot server. Won't glance toward the bartender. Won't betray myself to the suit. Somewhere. Who watches.

Ridges of swirls and whorls scrape against the table's mirrored plastic. I ride the last taste of a silk wave. Near the end of an unregistered sequence of artificial days and nights in a world that has neither naturally. Fear that I will revert to the pattern and not take the risk. Fear that I will risk and again fail.

"It has no corners!" The cowboy laughs, fashionably amused at his own punch line.

Silk pulls sound through me. Mingles it with the internal rhythm of the band's pounding music over the earvibe. Slow-motion moans from the orgasmic contortion on the wallscreen, bootlegged satellite sex from Earth. Intertwined conversations and real-time movement from the room, street, spinning station.

Blond hair curves around my face like a hood, ending even with my chin. Cowboy tells me I'm beautiful. Does he woo me with truth or a lie? At least I was born with a normal appearance. Spared the surgically perfect face and body the court would have ordered as part of my rights. Can't have our idiot genius looking mentally retarded, you know, someone might decide it was wrong to use her for high level work.

"Amanda," he says, a name I use more than others. He finds my inattentiveness chic. He thinks I look away and smile because he attracts me. The tips of my fingers, nails chewed to bleeding, travel through faint residue on the polished table. The absence of numbers puts the curve to my lips.

Numbers, curse of being a genius. Numbers and symbols for numbers. They grow in my head like vines, mental kudzu. Chocking all other thoughts. Only silk flutters them away.

Naked pornography blinks to an overdressed newscaster prepared to display a different set of distortions. Without slowing, the rhythm of the bar turns to the screen. All things from Earth are viewed with the same reverence. And skepticism.

"An unnamed source at the recently created Department of Space Exploration and Management reports that problems with the agency's new fluid computer have delayed the planned launch of the Pilgrim. A speaker for the department denies the report, saying that although problems do exist with the Ultra4, a back-up system is functioning as planned and the project is on schedule."

The natives listen while pretending not to. Most of Luna I-I is part of a chain reaction involving the spaceship. The only truly inattentive are the tourists. Cowboy.

"A poll conducted by our own network personnel shows that if the launch is delayed, public opinion will most likely turn against the staffed flight beyond our solar system. A successful launch is necessary to justify the department's formation and substantial budget."

A hum vibrates across my nerves, expected yet startling as a fulfilled wish. The robot server slides into my peripheral vision. I've practiced the art of seeing without looking, find it useful. The server delivers tall glasses. Red and black dance across the silvered curves. The names of the drinks we ordered print themselves on the machine's display along with the meaningless numbers of the tab. I battle the urge to look into my glass. Momentarily win. I offer to pay and cowboy is pleased.

I crush carefully folded bills into my palm. Feel the small lump wrapped in paper. Sound retreats until I grow deaf. Silk is the only courage I have. The only constant I value. A piece of blue tablet resides in the bills. Exorcist of demon numbers. My fingerprints seal the packet, thick so I'm sure the bartender is being sufficiently overpaid. I slip it into the slot on the server's belly.

The server glides to the next table. A chunk of blue freedom gone. Exchanged for a future. Numbers rattle outside my head like ghosts. I will not turn. I will not look at the bartender behind his acrylic barrier. If I do, my face will twist with pleading. And the suit will know. And the suit will stop me.

But if I hold still. Just hold still and believe that the bartender can be trusted to take the fragment of blue silk and store it in whatever secret place he has. Can be trusted to feed it back to me, coated enough so it won't dissolve until after my tolerance level for the lovely blue has dropped. As he has before, unsuccessfully. As I hope he has now, successfully. Just hold still and let the moment pass from silence—

Cowboy nudges my drink, trying to gently force a slug of alcohol through me, thinking inebriation will ignite into lust for his designer body.

Now I look. Now when it will not seem strange. Black liquid erupts with swirling red beads. And one bead. Larger than the rest. Surfaces and dives with the constant motion. The bartender is a saint. A god of salvation. I clink my glass to cowboy's. Savor the metallic ring as the large bead slides down my throat.

Music and voices rush through me. Relief spills from my mouth in laughter. "I'm a genius," I tell cowboy. Like Amanda, it's my own designation for myself. Not theirs. No. They believe me incapable of creative thought.

I lean close. "Which one is wearing the suit?" I sip my drink to expand his hope. Cowboy looks at me stupidly. I can't deal with stupid when I'm on silk.

"It's a game," I explain. "Ignore the clothes everyone is wearing." He likes that idea. "See them act, move, sit. Which one is really wearing a suit?" I keep my eyes on him while he watches the black and red dance hustlers, the black and red bar hustlers, the black and red drink hustlers. "That one." He nods toward a feather-capped dancer flying with the song, crest bobbing at the band suspended in its plastic cage.

Cowboy doesn't understand. Isn't interested in the game. Only in exploring my body. He's pretty the way an agate becomes smooth from much grooming. I want that prettiness while the silk still rolls in my blood, embracing me in blue folds.

He knows I'm won but he ignores it to prolong anticipation. To keep the night hot with crackling auras of close flesh.

He says rehearsed lines, adding inflected nuance, fabrication of depth. I respond, automatically spontaneous. He reaches the end of his flat wit and is in danger of falling off the edge. So we leave, stumbling along the tunnel through false gravity in the direction of his rented bed.

Away from the bar's holo-lighting our clothing rejects color and returns to white. Pale in the uneven pattern of glowing and perpetually broken lights.

A red and black hustler, the one who is really wearing a suit, steps through the portal after us. Turns colorless. Follows.

Unnatural lab light forces a squint. Sharp edged. Disturbing in its reluctance to form shadows. The fresh taste of silk is sweet on my tongue. At least Wickman didn't wake me in that terrible place he refers to as my room. He does that when he wants to annoy me. Everything contained in that rectangle is offensive. Overly padded furniture with flouncy coverings, grating primary colors, photographs of people I've never touched dangling from padded walls, frilly drapes framing a holo of a window that does not open. The illusion of a place for living, spotlighted by industrial fluorescence like the lab. No shadows. Flat. Without perspective.

I have no connection to that room. Not while silk rolls in smooth waves, billowing gossamer. And not while it doesn't.

The dull ache at my temples tells me the silk has been gone a long time. It moves sluggishly in my veins. "How long?"

Dr. Wickman's angular face flickers with a professional smile that is supposed to be warm, friendly. There must be someone else in the room. "Not long," he lies.

I force a meaningless random number into my head while I still can. "Eight days," I prod him so he'll choose a response close to the truth. Something went wrong. My mind aches and can't tell me.

"Little more than five." Another lie. "You know what five means, don't you?" he taunts. He propels an electronic pen across the sensitive surface of a personal notebook and does not look at me. I am too normal now to be of interest. He forgets to pretend for the other person.

"That's illegal." It was probably—a number forms, a silk wave rolls through my blood, the symbol vanishes unrecognized. Probably—more. More than what Wick says.

"You signed a consent form."

"That's a lie," I say because I want it to be a lie.

He grabs a sheet of smoke-thin permapaper, waves it in my face, lets it fall to my lap, a wounded butterfly.

The undersigned does hereby consent—

At the bottom is a thumbprint. Beside it, written in a precise scrawl, is the name my highly educated parents gave me before they turned me over to an institution that later sold me to the feds for a research grant.

"I'll contest it in court." I wasn't supposed to have signed this time. But I can't remember how I was going to stop myself, my other self, from doing whatever Wick instructed.

Wick smiles. Predator smile. He picks my bones to feed his insatiable craving. Eyes so calm there is no life behind them. Only dull hunger for the work.

Laws direct my existence. Enslave me and protect me with the same words. As incomprehensible as symbols. I'm incapable of using them to help myself. I can call up a lawyer's ID on the registry. I think I have. Sometime before. But while I'm on silk, symbols slide away without entering my mind, leaving my fingers without direction before the meaningless panel of the comm-net.

I rub my temples and blink away the ache. A squat, bearded man steps close, watches as if I were a rat that just ran a maze at the speed of light. Another doctor. "I hope you're a lawyer," I say, not allowing him to remain a detached observer.

"This is Dr. Delancy," Wickman says.

Delancy does nothing to acknowledge the introduction. This is not our first meeting, then. I chill, knowing what he saw. Before.

"Extraordinary," Delancy says. "I haven't worked with an autistic savant before. I wouldn't have believed it if—"

"If you hadn't seen the freak yourself," I finish for him. "This isn't an exhibition, Wickman. I'm not on display for your friends."

"Dr. Delancy has been directing you." Wick retrieves the untouched consent form from my lap. "He's coordinating the current phase of the project."

My stomach churns. How can this plump, soft man tolerate the near comatose thing that recites numbers? I cover my face against the stinging light. My hair falls forward, forming a globe.

Wickman taps my head until I look up. He hands me a familiar shiny box. I open the lid to be sure. Blue, curved waves that keep the silk rolling crowd together in the silver lining.

I snap it shut and press it into my palm.

"You didn't count the pills of course," Wick says, "but you recognized that I've given you the usual amount. I must inform you that apparently you've developed an increased tolerance for the neural suppressant. It's rare, but there are a few documented cases."

Rare—that's me.

"You returned hours earlier than usual," Wick says, "and you were in a significantly advanced condition."

"I'm not coming back." I smear my fingerprints across the silver box.

Wick ignores my declaration. "You were asleep on the tunnel floor at the lab entrance. Your fingernail scratches are in the lettering on the door."

Is he being cruel by lying or by telling the truth? I don't look at my ragged nails. Pink skin torn, stained with dried blood. "The suit screwed up then, can't even keep track of a retard in an orbiting station. You'd better hire a new one."

Wickman sighs. I have skewered a tender spot. "You have a right to know," he says.

"You're so careful with my rights. You and the suit." Invasion of privacy. Not allowed. Wick torments me with the rules he chooses to follow and the ones he ignores. In accordance with my rights, he shows me vids of my other self during "project sessions." Staring at nothing, responding with mechanical precision, gnawing at my fingernails, signing consent forms I do not comprehend. And in that horrid room with the padded walls, watching vids of old movies. The only memories I carry with me from my other self to this self.

He expects me to be grateful for the visions. Grateful for my periodic right to silk. My reward when he can no longer withhold it, when the "legal" consent forms that prolong the work sessions expire and he must grant it to me.

Wick is conscientious in his reminding me of all the disgusting details. So I'll understand, he says, about the blue pills, about having them and not having them, about the brain's tolerance level, about the cycle of so many days on and so many days off. About why I can't be on silk all the time.

Scratches in the door. Slashes through the stenciled letters. Truth or lie. How can I tell?

Delancy folds his arms across a wide chest that bulges his lab coat. "A circle has a radius of two centimeters. What is the area of the circle?"

"Wickman, get him away from me."

Wick doesn't budge, but at least Delancy is quiet.

"Your favorite band is playing at that bar you like to go to." Wickman is showing off for the new doctor. Tapping at my joints to demonstrate my reflexes.

The bar. Something went wrong. The bartender misjudged the amount of coating needed on the silk. I've no numbers to give him guidance. It attached itself to the wall of my stomach then dissolved too soon. Again. And my body rejected it. "That part of my life is off limits to you," I say. "You have no right to intrude."

"Of course."

Silk doesn't affect normal brains. There's no black market so the bartender has no reason to substitute something else and sell the silk.

And I believe I pay him very well to follow the instructions I slip into the robot server's slot along with the bills and chunks of blue.

Apparently I'm rich, but how can I tell? I only know that my account is never empty. The law prescribes that I be compensated according to my ability. What's a genius worth in the job market? I've read my own press. No one else—no other idiot savant—can do lightning calculations of complex equations as I can. A computer is only as good as its software. I'm hardwired from birth against error.

And a computer can't affect its own existence. I can.

When the bartender finally gets the amount of coating perfected, how long before Wick realizes I've cut a trap door through the side of the maze?

His confidence in the watchful suit will slow him down. His belief in his right to exploit me will keep him blind—

No. I don't lie to myself. At the first rebellion he'll know I'm no longer a passive rat. Then I must be more careful.

I'll still be imprisoned by silk and my body's tolerance level, by the cycle of on and off. Still enslaved. But within the parameters of slavery, I will wrest what control I can. I will take what there is to have.

I can't simply save a blue and hide it on my person. Once the affects begin to slip, once the waves begin to calm, I revert to that other self. Time compresses and the future is lost. I swallow my last grams without thought. I've never gotten as far as worrying about how to smuggle silk back into the complex, about finding a place to hide it in that monstrosity of a room until the immunity expires.

I can't hide it from my other self. I can't stop that person from sabotaging my own escape.

So I watched the movement of illegal commodities through the bar along with the other hustling. Watched without seeming to watch. And the bartender was the hub. I worked out a plan and made contact through the robot server. Right under the scrutiny of the suit.

Silk flows smoother now, and the initial disorientation eases. I ache to escape, but my legs feel wobbly, unable to support me.

Delancy is not the only new item in the room. There is also a board, the kind that can be written on then erased.

The soft-white surface holds rigid lines of numbers and the

symbols for numbers. Numbers and symbols. Numbers are symbols, and combinations of numbers and symbols mean other numbers, other symbols.

When I'm not on silk, the number-symbols push everything else from my mind until I'm no more real than they are, no more than a black scrawl in a formula.

Only silk rescues me, gives me breath. Makes me real again—as long as silk rolls.

"A markerboard. Is your new toy broken, Wick?" I know it's true, but I'm uncertain where the revelation came from. "Is that why you needed me for—" the number forms but escapes without my recognizing it, without my knowing what it symbolizes. "—for so many days?"

Wick's frown digs a deep channel between his heavy eyebrows. Delancy's round eyes are wide with surprise, as if the rat recited Shakespeare. "She understands—"

Wickman cuts him off with a waving hand. "It is only the temporary effect of the drug." But the movement is too frantic for Wick. He suddenly sees me as dangerous to his precious top-secret project. Silk gives me power. Would the media be interested in knowing that the leading computer scientist in the world—and beyond—has to have calculations done by hand because his computer is broken?

Delancy gazes at me with the soft puppy eyes of pity. "Then we should get her consent for the next phase now, while she can comprehend its importance."

"Already planning another extended session that breaks the law, Wick?" The thought shivers through the silk. I would not be aware while it was happening, would not remember afterward. But it would keep me in their maze longer and away from the blue folds.

Wick speaks calmly, an expert in the legalities of my

condition. "She's under the influence of a drug. Anything she signs now would be ruled illegal."

Delancy protests. "Without the drug she doesn't realize—"

Wickman swivels a dead stare to Delancy. "Doctor, this patient has been under my care and guidance for nine years, since she became eighteen and a court of law ruled it legal for the government to employ her for her specialty. She is an adult. According to the federal Balboa Act, no matter what her intelligence quotient or mental disability, she can enter into any contractual agreement she chooses. And according to federal law, a contractual agreement is illegal if one of the parties is under the influence of a non-medicinal substance. The neural suppressant is still experimental and therefore not recognized as of medical benefit."

The first part floats too far from my grasp, but I understand the rest. Wick is calling me stupid.

"A court would rule differently if it saw—" I let it fade, unable to speak of my other self in front of Wick.

"Perhaps. But there has been no test case involving the use of the neural suppressant on an autistic patient to set a legal precedent." Wick puts a hand on my shoulder. I cringe, but he clamps his fingers tight. "You could be the first. Of course, you would have to pass a drug test before filing your case. It's unlikely you'd be able to do both at the same time."

"Government logic," I say.

"Isn't the right to experimental products and procedures that might improve your condition worth a little incongruity? The government even supplies the neural suppressant."

"I earn my way."

"Yes, you're one of the few—" he pauses a beat. Delancy doesn't notice. I do. "—capable of contributing to the society that provides for your needs."

He means I'm one of the few of my kind. Prodigious savant. Rare of the rare. How disappointed the scientific community must have been when it discovered me. Ladies and gentlemen, we have good news and bad news. The good news: We have found a human brain capable of performing mathematical calculations better than our best computer. The bad news: That's the only thing this brain can do.

"I'm not coming back," I say.

"That's your right, of course."

Wick doesn't believe me. Do I say this every time?

I walk out of the lab on uncertain legs. Sound comes to me. Makes me transparent. The buzz of the harsh lights crackles through me. In the long gray tunnel that connects the government research section to the rest of the orbiting complex I don't look at the door. I don't want to know if there are fingernail scratches through the stenciled letters.

The ache in my head is enormous. I hold very still to avoid vomiting. Perspiration slides from my upper lip into my mouth in salty drops. I keep my eyelids clenched tight against the blast of fluorescent light. Only a negative image, like the holo effect in a bar I know, registers. A round face, puppy eyes, bow mouth pushed into a frown by pouchy cheeks.

The nausea eases as silk drapes over me. Lightly I touch a wrist. Clammy but real skin. Not the rubbery falseness of surgical adhesive holding flaps of tissue together like the last time I came to the silk feeling this bad. Wickman was very angry with me for trying to kill myself. I was angrier with myself for failing. He kept me from silk for a long time after that. My body horribly rejected it when the blue wave finally rolled through my blood. Coaxing. Coaxing until I relaxed into its folds.

Beneath the ridges on my fingertip I trace the thin line of the old scar. The memory of failure keeps me from trying again. So far.

"Are you all right?" says the negative image on my eyelids.

"How long?" My body tells me it has been very long.

"Fifteen days."

The truth, although I don't comprehend it. Delancy then. A sip of clear water touches my lips and I drink, relishing the aftertaste of sweet silk that lingers from a previous swallow.

"Don't baby her, Dr. Delancy. She's not a child." Wick's voice.

I sigh down to my soul. Another chunk of blue, encased in red and swallowed with a Lunar Blast, wasted. Another piece of freedom lost. The casing, thicker than before, still dissolved too quickly, releasing silk before my tolerance level fell.

"I'm not coming back," I whisper through silk. "I'm not coming back."

I lunge from the room as soon as my legs can support me and stagger through the internal design of boxes and hallways to the stenciled door. The gray tunnel provides only one way to go, but I'm grateful for that. Behind me I hear Delancy's squeaky shoes and labored breathing as he tries to catch up.

I wait for him before the juncture to the main tunnel. Somewhere in the confusion of shops and bars and too many people in too small a space the suit watches for me to turn that corner. I prefer the suit not see the lab-coated doctor flapping after me.

Delancy puffs and grabs his chest. He is slightly taller than I am. His puppy-pity eyes look down at me. "I'm not sure you'll understand any of this, but you should know—" The pity is really for himself. For being in this position. For having to behave in a way that is ethically correct so he can salvage his view of himself as human.

"I'm not an idiot. Not at the moment." I would never say that in front of Wickman.

Delancy gasps in a breath. He doesn't appreciate my humor. "The new computer—"

"The Ultra," I say impatiently. He does think of me as an idiot, but at least a human idiot.

"Ultra4. Yes. It works fine for a while and then it comes up with answers that mostly make sense but that are a little off. It's hard to determine which parts are wrong."

"And Wickman is having me do the same calculations so he can find out when the computer's answers are correct and when they're not." Did he think I was completely unaware of what I'd been doing most of my life? "That's my job. Wick always uses me to verify new equipment and new software."

Delancy looks at the floor and shakes his head. "He's abandoned the computer entirely. He's using us—you—to work through all the equations for the Pilgrim's flight. Our—your—calculations are being programmed into the computer on the ship."

"I don't care if he recites them to monkeys," I say. "Now there's a bar waiting for me."

He grabs my arm, stops me from turning away. "That ship must not be sent into space. The safety of the people on board depends on the Ultra4 and a reliable link between it and the Pilgrim's computer. Sometimes the fluid computer completely refuses to acknowledge the Pilgrim. What if that happens during the flight? I've tried to explain it to the agency, but Wickman tells them I'm exaggerating. They listen to him, not to me."

"So you want the genius retard to tell them?" I laugh. Hysteria, honed by the loss of the red-coated silk scrapes along the molded walls. I shudder as a blue wave pulls the sound back through me.

"No. No." He releases me. "You have a gift."

"Would you want it?"

"There's no person who can take your place, and the Ultra4 is just as specialized a computer. Even dividing the tasks among a dozen of the military's high-powered machines can't duplicate the Ultra, when it functions correctly. The company is building another, but it won't be ready until after all launch windows are closed."

"So you'll help me run away."

Delancy nods. "I'll get you enough NS so you don't have to come back."

"Not ever?" His naive ethics are maddening. He's going to rescue me and save the world. I relish the marvelous impossibility of it. "What about in between? Will you take care of me while my tolerance level is too high for the—the NS to be effective?"

Delancy bites the lower lip of his little bow mouth. He hasn't thought this through. But I have.

He sags against the curved plastic, deflated, too tired to lie to either of us. During the past days of my captivity in the lab he wrote the maze of complicated equations on the markerboard, placed my other self at the entrance, encouraged me along the route to reach the cheese. For every unregistered day I worked during the last, long, session, so did he. He's earned the exhaustion. "We must prevent the work from being completed, leave the equations unsolved. Wickman cannot be allowed to play with people's lives."

Is Delancy's concern exclusively for the crew of the Pilgrim or does it include me?

"I'll figure out a way," Delancy says. "Dr. Wickman told me about that bar you go to. I'll meet you there. Tonight."

"Don't come too late." Poor Delancy. Enlisting me as his only ally. "I expect to line up some other entertainment for later on." I laugh at the sober way he accepts that. He doesn't have a clue what I mean.

"You will call me Amanda," I tell Delancy as he sits beside me. I push a throat-scorching drink at him and sip my Blast.

The round doctor squirms against cushioned plastic. The red and black lighting reacts violently to his patterned jacket, which delights the other patrons, ghostly white beneath the projected colors. A few of the males scowl. I had great fun reserving the chair for Delancy. The rejected males are disappointed by the doctor's pudginess, having convinced themselves that only Adonis could succeed where they had failed. They will recover quickly.

"Thank you for meeting me." Delancy darts a nervous glance at the mixed crowd of laborers and tourists. At the crash and burn band thrashing in its acrylic cage, and almost chocks. At the naked bodies on the wallscreen, and almost faints. This is not his element.

"I've worked something out," he says. "The first opportunity to launch the ship has already past." His exhausted condition has increased since our conversation in the tunnel. He moves in quick twitches, jacked up on adrenaline and intrigue.

"The primary window." Anyone, even an idiot, who lives on an orbiting launch pad knows the jargon. Before hitting the bar, I viewed all the news reports since my last time out, working from a marker I set because I can't go by date. Plus, an account of the asteroid dispute that went on longer than the dispute itself, a novel about a young woman who is self-destructive because her father died when she was a child, and a collection of tolerable contemporary sonnets.

Delancy recognizes my knowledge with a nod. "If the secondary window is missed, the launch will be postponed indefinitely. The agency will conduct an inquiry. The severity of the problem will be discovered, and Dr. Wickman will be reprimanded for actions that would have endangered the crew of the Pilgrim.

He grips the glass like salvation and leans close against the noise. "You can make Wickman miss the timeline. You can slow his progress by not consenting to anymore extended work sessions."

Simple. He thinks saying it makes it possible. I wish he would use my name. I wish he would look at me and see Amanda. "Now, Delancy, you must learn to pay more attention to what goes on around you. Without the—" I almost call it silk, but that's my private title for it "—neural suppressant, I'll sign anything. And with it I can't legally protest."

"At the end of your tolerance cycle I'll slip you a dose of NS. Then when Dr. Wickman puts the consent form in front of you, you refuse to sign. All you have to do is pretend that you're still—well—" He blushes red and black. "You know what I mean."

Silk, as soon as my body can accept it. Guaranteed. No guessing how thick to make the red coating. No ache because time on the blue waves was stolen from me. The work slows down and I get silk on schedule.

I sip my Blast, swallowing the gritty red rocks. There's nothing extra hidden in them. It would be too soon. I simply drink Blasts all the time so the suit won't get suspicious. "And when we're successful, when the launch is cancelled, you'll continue to provide me with the NS."

Delancy's eyes get very round. His mouth oscillates between open and closed. A fish suddenly on sand, starving for oxygen despite the air around it. He wants to tell the truth. But the rat must believe in the reward at the end of the maze or it won't bother. "Yes," he says. "Of course." He smiles with his lips, but the lie never reaches his puppy eyes. "I'll be ready at the end of your next tolerance cycle. I'm sure I can get a dose by then."

Behind the plastic barrier, streaked red and black, a thin young man in transparent briefs and a star-burst slashed tank top throws his voice and body into a song. Around him musicians pound out the accompaniment. "I'm not going back," I sing to the band's clash in my earvibe.

"Next time," Delancy says. "I promise."

I take out the vibe and watch the singer's silent screaming. He throws himself to the stage floor and writhes in torment.

Delancy stands to leave. I'm disappointed that he hasn't tasted his drink. I chose the noxious stuff so carefully, an effort to get him aligned with the environment. "You'd better have a good story ready for the suit," I tell him. He doesn't understand. Used to privilege, he thinks being an ignorant genius will protect him. It hasn't done much for me.

The robot server hums over with another drink. I switch empty for full. The server's monitor displays the meaningless symbols of the tab. I take the prepared bills from my pocket. Press them into my palm until I feel the lump wrapped inside. Slide the packet into the slot. Whatever else happens, the actions, and the hope, are part of my routine now.

I place the vibe back in my ear for mercy. Isolation broken, the band is less terrifying to watch. Disjointed chords dance together. The hidden rhythm consumes.

A man steps up to my table. Glass held crotch level as is the style. Suave, romantic comedy type. Practiced vulnerability in his slight smile. "Is your friend coming back?"

I shrug. "He abandoned me."

He sits down, smoothly, weightlessly. "Maybe you need a new friend."

The bar vibrates with neon butterflies. I collect them and hold them inside me, savoring the warm flutter of wings.

Butterflies stir from sleep in a blue wave, a silky blue wave, scattering numbers. And I feel good. I feel so very good.

Fluorescent glare bounces from the smeared markerboard. Delancy, marker in hand, grins, barely able to hide the triumph, bites his lip in warning.

Remember. Hold still and remember. Delancy came through on time. Silk flows effortlessly through my blood. I lock my eyes on the floor, clench fists against my chest. I know what I must do. I've seen the vids, those terrible vids that show how numbers torment me. Numbers and the symbols for numbers.

I shove fingers in my mouth and gnaw on my nails. Gently rock, gently rock.

The sound of a door and footsteps flood into me. Wickman's footsteps.

"Is there a problem, Dr. Delancy?"

"She has become inattentive."

"Then you must get her attention back," Wickman says. I thought he only used that calm, mocking tone with me.

Delancy clunks the marker into a tray at the bottom edge of the board. "No need. The session is nearly over anyway."

Wickman hisses in a slow breath. He's used to being obeyed. Used to others believing, as he does, that the project—whatever it happens to be at the moment—is the only priority. "Of course you realize that the equation you're working on is at a critical stage and cannot easily be dropped then picked up three days from now." He reaches into a file drawer, pulls out a filmy piece of permapaper and attaches it to his clipboard. He scratches at it with a pen then holds it out to Delancy. "I'm sure you agree, doctor, that the session must be extended."

The room suddenly has no sound except Wickman's voice.

"I've filled in the date and the time. Now that you are officially her doctor of record, the form requires your signature."

Delancy controls the forms; he controls the silk! Deception is unnecessary. So why—?

Delancy stares at the paper, on the edge of comatose.

I scream at him to laugh in Wick's face. But all is silence.

Wickman's arm grows tired. "Come now, Dr. Delancy. This is my project. You still work for me."

Delancy signs, presses his thumb against the filmy paper. I rock, rock. The room implodes with sound. We each take what power we can, in whatever subversive forms we can. I hate Delancy for signing; I love him for the silk.

Delancy shoves the clipboard back at Wickman. Wick smiles, satisfied with his power. "See the clock?" Wick says to me. "It's time to write your name on the paper."

He forces the pen into my fist and slides the clipboard into my line of sight. Delancy's cowardice is written in plump letters above the line marked with an X that waits for my other name.

"No," I say.

Wickman staggers back as if dowsed with cold water. He shakes his head, angry with himself for reacting. He steps close to me, clipboard ready. "See the numbers on the clock?" he says soothingly. "You always sign the paper at fifty-five minutes after the hour."

I follow his pointing finger to the digital readout on the wall. Remnants of numbers flicker in my head. I've watched a similar scene on vid. This one will have a different ending.

He swivels his pointing finger to me and taps my fist clenching the pen, a tap for each word. "Now it's time to sign."

"No."

"She refused, doctor. Twice," Delancy says, rejoining the living. "According to the articles of the Balboa Act—"

"I don't need you to quote me the law," Wickman shouts. He frowns and looks back and forth between us. I rock and rock. Delancy stands so rigid I fear he'll shatter.

Wickman clatters the clipboard onto his desk and slowly forms his predator smile. "Take good care of your patient, Dr. Delancy," Wick says and stalks from the lab.

Delancy blanches. His eyelids twitch as if his spirit is going to leave again, but he hangs on.

Wickman knows. And is more dangerous because of it.

Delancy and I give one another furtive warning looks. A lighted square glows on a panel of squares. Cameras record our movements, so the celebration will have to wait. We go through the routine. He pretends to give me another dose of silk and I pretend to accept its influence.

Following my usual pattern, I leave the lab and go to the

public comm-net area to review the news that passed while I existed as my other self. There is less volume than usual, which reaffirms the euphoria I've felt since the beginning of the silk. Delancy slipped the blue wave to me right at the end of my tolerance cycle. No rejection. No ache. A smooth transition into gossamer folds.

I have what I want. Delancy has what he wants. According to the recorded newscaster, the Pilgrim missed its primary window due to "unforeseen difficulties" with the Ultra-whatsit. The next launch date is given, incomprehensible to me. The newscaster describes it as "early within the secondary window."

I let the vid run. The reporter is handsome in a granite-faced way. Sculpted by an artist. Surgically perfect.

And if Delancy and I manage to continue the charade until that window closes too—then what?

". . . experts have been added to the ship's crew in case problems arise after the launch," says the screen image through the earvibe.

More people on Delancy's conscience.

Once the crew of the Pilgrim is safe, will he continue to stretch his humanitarian streak so that it touches me?

In the subdued public comm-net area I devour Jung, Chekov, Hesse, and a play in the new deltan style destined to remain obscure. Tiny sounds float through me, whispered politeness, considerate isolation, shared respect. What does the suit do while I read?

Stronger in spirit, I wander to the bar, uncertain if I will slip a packet to the bartender.

Numbers tag symbols then run away. Symbols melt to a blur.

Silk rolls strong. Strong. I squint at the harsh light.

Wickman watches me, arms folded across his chest. Delancy stutters over an equation. Tries again. Gets mired in the gibberish and gives up.

"Something wrong, Dr. Delancy?" Wickman asks, his eyes on me.

Delancy pinches the skin between his eyebrows. "I'm tired. I need a break."

I must remember something. I hold still. Numbers dance at the edge of my mind. I feel good. I feel good and the numbers scatter.

Delancy is flushed, perspiring. I stare at the floor, clench fists to my chest, rock back and forth. Back and forth. Wickman knows.

A paper is already on the clipboard. Wickman picks it up from his desk. "I have a consent form for you to sign," he says to me. "The same kind you always sign."

A lie. I didn't sign it last time.

"Only there is one small difference."

Delancy blots his sleeve against his forehead. Is the man sick?

"This one allows you to go on a trip. Remember, you signed a paper so you could travel from Earth to here. This paper says you can go on another trip, to another place where you will live for a while."

I tuck my chin into my chest. Leave? Just when I'm making progress here. Delancy. The bartender. I rock faster, unable to slow myself. Is this a trick?

"And Dr. Delancy is going along to help you with your work."

Delancy doesn't look well enough to go anywhere.

"Come now," Wickman coos, taping me on the head with a

finger. "You'll have your exact same room."

A vision of a phony window and phony photographs makes me nauseous. He's pushing so I'll break. I stare and rock back and forth. Back and forth. I've seen the vids. I know my other self. The square is lit. I'm being recorded. A legal record.

"We'll just move your entire room to the ship."

Ship. So Delancy and I are the experts mentioned in the newscast. To act as backup in case the Ultra refuses to talk to the Pilgrim during flight. Astrophysicist and his idiot savant lightning calculator.

"You'll like the Pilgrim. Lots of nice people will live there with you, and you'll have Dr. Delancy to take care of you. You count on the doctor to take care of you, don't you? And he counts on you to help him when he has a problem too difficult to solve by himself."

Bastard. I hear you Wickman. Delancy is using me to save the Pilgrim because it means saving himself.

Bastards.

"Watch, I'll have Dr. Delancy sign first." He presents the clipboard and pen to Delancy with a slight bow as if bestowing an award.

Delancy grasps his potential future in quivering hands. Blood rushes from his face, leaving him ghostly and wavering.

Wickman focuses on me. He's testing. Testing.

Don't do it, Delancy, I scream through silence. Feel your power. Take control. Don't run the maze.

Delancy's plump fingers jiggle the pen across the paper. He presses his thumb into the sensitive rectangle. His puppy eyes full of self-pity. Self-loathing. Defeat. He looks to me with hope. I'm to save him when he didn't save himself. I can't tolerate stupid while I'm on silk. I can't stand self-pity and helplessness.

Wickman retrieves the clipboard and pen before they slip from Delancy's hands. "You see, your friend Dr. Delancy knows that this project is important and should not be halted because of one person's unfounded fears."

He believes it. His work is the only philosophy he knows, his only god, his only ethic.

He puts the clipboard in front of my stare, holds the pen out to me. But I've seen the vids. He made sure I saw the vids.

"No," I say.

Wickman smiles without surprise. Delancy takes a prolonged breath, wipes his face with a corner of his lab coat.

"Perhaps I didn't explain it clearly enough," Wickman says.

"It isn't time," I say. "The paper doesn't come until—" I have no numbers. I cross my arms tighter over my chest. Back and forth. Back and forth. I have no numbers. I'll betray myself, and my actions will be ruled invalid. "—until the clock says it's time."

"And what time is that?" Wickman asks, waving the clipboard before my staring eyes.

"Doctor." Delancy puts a hand on Wickman's shoulder. Wickman turns sharply and knocks it aside. He doesn't like to be touched because it implies power. Because it's how he shows me he's in control.

Delancy's fear is white on his cheeks, but he can taste victory and it makes him bold. "Dr. Wickman, you know that forcing an autistic patient to act outside of a set routine can trigger a violent episode." Delancy deflects Wick with doctor talk. Reminding him I'm not a person with a name. I'm a patient with a named condition, incapable of acting without a given direction. Incapable of engineering my own maze. "It is now less than 45 seconds until five minutes to the hour, when the consent form is usually presented to the patient. Surely you can wait that long."

The numbers on the wall progress without me. Delancy smiles at the clock. "There. Now everything is in order."

I blink and focus on the paper. Wickman slides the pen into my fist.

Carefully, routinely, I write the terrible words my parents gave my other self before they turned me over to the feds. Precisely on the line with the X at the beginning, forming each letter as I do every time. Then I press my right thumb against the heat sensitive rectangle beside the name, as I always do.

Delancy stands bleached and trembling, eyes staring, mouth opening and closing without a sound.

Wickman takes the document and pen. I expect a gloat but his face is sober. He touches a lighted square. It turns dark. The cameras have stopped.

"It isn't legal," Delancy whispers. "She's on NS. I gave it to her myself."

"Come now, Dr. Delancy. You must focus on the greater good. The Pilgrim's flight benefits all human kind." Wickman doesn't look at his colleague. He files the permapaper consent form and begins making notations as he always does at the end of a session.

"I'm not coming back," I say.

"Of course," Wick says.

28

Jonah

The story has been wrongly told,
for I am witness, cursed to speak.
In the flowing desert where wind
builds ageless sculptures in fluid sand
then drains them down to rocky core,
great ribs emerged from arid waves,
curved pillars of Leviathan, cradling
man-sized bones and a human skull.

The Universe Seen as a Floating Orange Rind

Knock, knock
Who's there?
Your creation
My creation who?

> Fourteen million nine hundred and twenty-nine thousand four hundred and sixth millennium Granite philosopher

At the age of thirty-one Albert Wren was abandoned, with good cause, by his mother. Considering Albert's personality, it's amazing she didn't do so earlier, a fact that qualifies her for sainthood. If Albert had been an enslaved Israelite in Egypt, Moses would have left him behind. And if there had been more forethought put into it, an eleventh commandment would have been written specifically for Albert beginning with "Thou shalt not" and concluding with something like "inflict thy dependency upon the innocent."

Saint or not, Albert's mother had no intention of carrying her burden to the grave, thereby becoming a martyr. Having a comprehensive understanding of her son's nature, she realized that the easiest way to sever one tie was to create another. She therefore sent an unemployed, broke Albert to an aunt in Minneapolis who, in her estimation, was crazy anyway. A perfect solution.

"Albert!" The woman flung her scrawny bird-like arms about him and pressed her soft cheek against his, making little kissing sounds, first one side and then the other. "It's been so long! Where have you been hiding yourself? Off on one of your little junkets again?"

Albert wasn't sure what his aunt meant by that. He felt awkward standing in the doorway of her expensive Lake Harriet home in dirty jeans and a crumpled canvas jacket over a faded plaid shirt like a begging poor relation. Which, he realized, he was.

Although Albert didn't really know his great aunt, her greeting left no doubt as to who she was. It did, however, make him wonder how she knew who he was after about thirty years. He must have changed at least a little since he was a baby. Maybe, Albert speculated, after his mother phoned Aunt Frederica and told her he was coming, she started calling every male who came to the door Albert. Unsure of what to say, he managed a simple, "Hello, Aunt Frederica."

"Frederica? Why, Albert, you know I haven't used that name in ever so long." She ushered him into a large sitting room packed with rich wood furniture, original paintings in carved frames, an oriental rug, and brass accents. The odor of exotic tea swirled through the air. "Sabrina, I go by Sabrina now and have for some time. Why just last—, or was it two months ago? I don't remember. Well, the important thing is you called me Aunt Sabrina then, so you should be able to remember to call me Aunt Sabrina now."

"But, Aunt—ah, Sabrina, I haven't seen you in over thirty years, not since I was a baby."

"Nonsense." She brushed aside his confusion as if it were a mosquito. "We see one another all the time. Why, you always come and tell me about the house." She sat down on a gold brocade settee and patted the cushion. Hesitantly, he perched beside her, aware of his gritty jeans on the immaculate upholstery.

"The house on Marshall Street, that house?" Was his aunt clairvoyant? She certainly looked it in her flowing gypsy skirt and paisley shawl. Heavily made-up green eyes twinkled in her small oval face. A multicolored scarf wrapped around her head and tied behind the left ear covered all except a large golden earring and a curly strand of bright red hair. If a crystal ball suddenly floated by, he wouldn't have been surprised—not too surprised anyway.

No, his mother must have mentioned the house when she called Aunt Frederica to make sure she was still alive, so Albert wouldn't be making the trip from Tacoma to Minneapolis for nothing. Or maybe she had him confused with someone else, a gardener or caretaker maybe. That would make this more complicated.

"Of course, the house on Marshall Street," she said. "What other house would we discuss?"

"Actually, I did want to talk about the house, the one on Marshall Street." He cleared his throat and went into the speech he had rehearsed on the bus most of the way from

Washington. "You know, a house shouldn't sit empty. It isn't good for insurance rates and—and things. And I was wondering, mother and I were wondering—"

"Your mother!" Albert jumped back from his aunt's reaction and felt the curved arm of the settee cut into his back. His aunt's bird hands fluttered and her voice became low and mystical.

"You've talked to her?"

"Of course," Albert squeaked out. "She suggested that I—"

"Aha!" his aunt roared triumphantly. Then she dropped her voice to a whisper and leaned close to Albert, as if they were secret conspirators. "Your mother called me on the telephone, that's how she always speaks to me. She told me I would be seeing you very soon. And all this time you thought I was losing my mind. Well, now she's contacted you, too."

His mother had said Aunt Frederica was more than a little strange. Albert wasn't sure what he had expected, but this wasn't it. No wonder his mother had given up trying to communicate regularly with her years ago. He stood to distance himself from his aunt's curious behavior and to get his concentration back on his mission.

"About the house," Albert tried again. "I've had a few setbacks lately—they're only temporary. But until I can get on my feet again I thought if I could live at the house and keep it fixed up, that maybe you wouldn't mind?" he asked hopefully. His palms were sweaty, and he discovered he had been wringing his hands during the oration. He knew he had said everything much too fast, and he hoped she wouldn't ask him to repeat it.

His aunt stared at him as if looking for a crack or chip, some sign that he was disintegrating. "Why would I mind now, if I didn't mind before? Honestly, Albert, sometimes I don't know what you're talking about."

Abruptly, she got up and walked over to the large picture window almost totally obscured by floor to ceiling glass shelving filled with plants. She picked up a brass watering can and began tending to a large, lacy fern. As if they had been discussing the subject all along she said, "Do you think the kitchen should be painted?"

Albert was about to say that since he hadn't seen the kitchen, any kitchen, he couldn't give an opinion. But since he thought she might have just given him permission to live in the house, it wouldn't hurt to humor her, even call her Sabrina if that's what she wanted. "You're absolutely right, Aunt Sabrina, the kitchen definitely needs painting." Now if he could just get some money.

His aunt went to an ornate glass-doored cabinet and pulled out a massive, black leather-bound Bible. "Let me see," she said thoughtfully, "Paul to Timothy: 'The love of money is the root of all evil.'"

Albert cringed at the quote.

From among the parchment pages she pulled out a crisp hundred-dollar bill. Handing it to him she said, "Get what you need with this. Since you live there, it's best if you pick out the color yourself."

Albert stared at the bill in his hand, amazed at how light it felt. Such an important piece of paper should have more density to it. "I'll need a key to the house," he finally managed to say. He hoped that wasn't being too pushy.

"You've lost your key again, have you?" Sabrina asked, unconcerned. "Why don't you just use the one in the bird feeder until you can get a new one made. That's what you usually do."

"What I usually—?" Albert started, then caught himself. "Oh, yes," he said slowly and carefully, nodding his head to show her that of course she made perfect sense and he agreed with everything, anything, she said. "I'll use the one in the bird feeder. Why didn't I think of that."

Out in the hallway the grandfather clock struck the hour in long, resonant bongs that vibrated through the floor and made the room rattle.

"You'll have to leave now, Albert dear," his aunt informed him. "It's four o'clock, time to practice my ballet."

Setting his brush so it hung over the edge of the counter, Albert stood back and surveyed his work. The freshly applied olive green paint covered two-thirds of the kitchen wall. The remaining one-third was still the old dirty-yellow it must have been for a decade or more. Albert's inexperience with a brush showed in the sporadic flecks of yellow showing through the green, and the jagged frontier of new paint where the wall met the ceiling.

"Yuk," Albert said, not feeling very well himself after breathing paint fumes while slurping beer.

The paint was on sale. It was all Albert could afford after buying groceries, beer, and socks with the money his aunt had given him. He felt guilty about using some of the cash for his personal needs and even guiltier about first considering not painting the kitchen at all and keeping the entire hundred for himself. His aunt would never know the difference, he reasoned, so what harm would it do?

Then he saw the terrible condition of the house his aunt owned on Marshall Street. He started feeling sorry for the rich, nutty old lady who didn't have anyone to help her take care of her own property. His mother would be glad to know that all of her guilt training had fallen on fertile ground.

The hardware store was about to close when Albert finally got there. But he was determined to commit himself to the task before he could talk himself out of it. The clerk didn't try to hide his annoyance at a late customer, and Albert had to load the paint into the trunk of Aunt Sabrina's Mercedes by himself.

A late evening breeze reluctantly drifted in through an open window making the air colder but no more breathable. Albert was beginning to feel nauseous.

"Is this being turned into a military instillation?"

Albert jumped at the voice behind him, knocking the brush off the counter with a wet slap and a trail of drab green splotches leading to an irregular dark rectangle on the greasy, checkered linoleum. He grabbed the brush off the floor and spun into a crouch, menacingly pointing the paintbrush at the intruder.

The old man, long white hair flowing over his shoulders, squinted at Albert. "You're not going to say bang, are you?"

"Who are you?" Albert demanded.

"I don't want to play games, Albert." His appearance was old, his voice ancient. "It's a long trip here, and I had to share a pod with a Gsff," he made a sneezing sound. "They have no flare for conversation, and they act as if the existence of every other species in the universes is a personal insult."

"How do you know my name? How did you get in here?" Albert waved the brush gut level at the old man's creased white tunic.

"Is this your way of telling me that the report you were supposed to have finished two of your months ago is not yet ready?" he said sharply, hands on his hips. "I've stalled The

Center as long as I can. You've got to complete that report."

Albert didn't understand what the strange geezer in the floor-length dress was talking about. He could see that the man was not intimidated by a paintbrush dripping olive green into a puddle on the floor. Unable to think of anything else, Albert decided to try logic.

"Listen, you must have me confused with someone else, some other Albert who looks like me who was maybe taking care of this place for a while."

"That seems unlikely," the old man said indignantly.

"Yes, it does," Albert had to agree.

"It seems much more likely that you are exactly who I think you are. Albert Wren, thirty-one years old, unmarried—although you're long past the standard age when such ritual usually occurs for your species—living off your one surviving parent and your aunt, who owns this house."

"How—how—how," Albert stammered, thinking that the only things the old man left out were the dark birthmark on his thigh and that he'd been fired from his job as a radio announcer for making an innocent comment on the air about a female Jell-O wrestler.

"I told you, Albert, I know you."

"But I don't know you."

The old man sighed. "Does that mean I don't get the report?"

"What report?"

"Oh, Albert!" he said with all patience lost. Reaching a hand to his ear, he gave two quick tugs and disappeared.

Albert blinked several times and gave his head a shake. I have to get some fresh air, he told himself. These paint fumes are getting to me.

The next morning Albert still felt disoriented from his visit with Aunt Frederica-Sabrina and from the paint-fume hallucination. When the phone rang, he jumped, surprised that it was even connected. "Hello?" he said, expecting it to be a wrong number.

"All right, Wren, where is she?" the deep, gruff voice demanded.

Albert could imagine the person on the other end: six-six; linebacker's neck; burly chest; dark, hooded eyes; jagged scar across the left cheekbone; swastika on his chain-draped, black leather jacket; a locker room odor hovering around him.

"Mr. Wren is not at home at the moment." Albert tried to say calmly but his voice suddenly became adolescent and uncontrollable.

"And who are you, his fruity butler?"

"Would you like to leave a message?" Albert asked, not as smoothly as he'd hoped to.

The low rumbling laughter that answered sent a chill through Albert's spine. "Listen, Wren, kick my old lady out of your bed and send her home or I'll come over there and shove a Buick down your throat."

Albert told himself to stay calm as he shakily hung up the phone. The call must have been a wrong number. Albert hadn't even dated a woman since—since—he couldn't remember. Yet the beast called him by name. Albert had just moved in. He wasn't even in the phonebook. The phonebook!

Aunt what's-her-name seemed to keep a strange collection of things at the house. Albert rummaged around in what appeared to be the catch-all drawer and came up with a year-old phone directory.

He searched out the 'W's. Instead of finding some small

verification of his sanity, he discovered "Wren, Albert" with the same telephone number after it as the one printed on the old-fashioned dial before him.

Albert went to the window and pulled back the thin faded drapes to stare through dusty glass at the quiet residential street. It was the kind of neighborhood where people jogged in the early morning, children rode bicycles and people curbed their dogs. Not the kind of neighborhood where strangers threatened you with Buicks and old men popped in and out of your kitchen.

Paint fumes could explain the little old man, but not the phone call. Albert wondered if he'd imagined it, and the telephone listing too. But that would make him crazy. And he wasn't crazy two days ago when he got here, at least, he didn't think so.

Coincidence, Albert thought. These freakish things happen. He slowly said the word out loud, "Co-in-ci-dence."

"No such thing," a familiar, wizen voice said from the direction of a fuzzy overstuffed chair.

Albert slapped a hand across his eyes and held very still. Slowly he spread apart his fingers and twisted his head around to peer at the chair.

"Peek-a-boo, Albert," the old man said sarcastically.

Albert looked frantically around the room then back to the relic seated comfortably in his living room.

"What's the matter?" the old man asked. "Don't remember where you put your loaded paintbrush? Maybe you hid it by your bed in case burglars break in while you're asleep."

"Are you going to ask about the report again?" Albert demanded. Having a phantom show up at night was one thing, but seeing him in full daylight before lunch was almost too much to handle.

"I was hoping to work it into the conversation," the old man replied. "You've put me in a very bad position, Albert. It's the end of the fiscal millennium and I need that report."

"I'll have to move back in with my mother," Albert mumbled to himself, closing his fingers over his eyes again.

"Your mother is dead," the old man said as if it were a commonly known bit of information. "She and your brother Tony died in a train wreck in India when you were six months old."

Albert took his hand away from his face. At least this guy doesn't know everything. "It was my father who died in that train wreck," he said boldly. "My father is dead."

The old man shrugged, "Don't tell him that, he'll get very upset." He walked over and touched Albert on the shoulder. For looking and sounding so decrepit, he moved with remarkable agility. "What happened to your protector shield?"

Albert looked at him without comprehension. The old man touched him again. Albert felt a slight tingle travel over his body then dissipate.

"You really don't know who I am?" the old man asked.

"No," Albert said sharply, angered at the comments about his father and at the stranger's know-it-all attitude.

"Faddle."

"What?"

"Faddle, that's my name. And you really don't know why I'm here or what report I'm asking for?"

"No."

Faddle stared intently at Albert's face. "I believe you."

Albert's relief lasted only a moment. "Great, the person who believes me is a figment of my imagination."

"A fig? Oh, pretend!" Faddle shook his head at the silliness of such an idea. "There's no such thing as make believe, Albert," he said as if Albert were a child. "Everything is real."

Albert was not comforted by the thought.

"Aunt Sabrina, has anyone else been using the house? Anyone besides me?" Albert shouted over the snappy Charleston scratched out by the Victrola.

"Well, I'm sure you'd know that better than I." She swung her spindly legs forward and backward, making her short, beaded chemise rattle rhythmically. In the black and white dress and with the wide black band around her short blond hair she looked like an aging flapper straight out of a speak-easy.

"There's this man. He's short, long gray hair, wears a white toga kind of thing. Do you know anyone like that?" Albert had returned the Mercedes, using it as an excuse to visit his aunt. He was sitting on the edge of a footstool covered with needlepoint flowers in vivid reds and violets. With most of the furniture piled around the perimeter of the room, it was the only place he could find to sit. The whole room was scented with summer jasmine. To his left a free-standing ice bucket held a chilled bottle of champagne. Next to it the record player perched on a low table that balanced on a high chest.

The music ended. Sabrina took the needle off the vinyl and fanned her face with a graceful hand. "That sounds like Mr. Faddle," she said pouring two long-stemmed glasses to the brim with champagne and offering one to Albert, "your employer. Cheers!" They clicked glasses. Sabrina drained hers in one swig.

Albert was mid-gulp when he realized what she had said.

He choked on the bubbles and came up coughing.

"You should take care of that cold, dear," Sabrina said pouring herself more wine and topping off Albert's glass before he had a chance to protest. "Better than coffee," she commented. "No caffeine."

"Aunt Sabrina, I don't have an employer. I don't even have a job."

"Of course, you do. That research job for Mr. Faddle."

"Have you actually met this Faddle person?"

"No, of course not, but you've told me all about him. Maybe you should invite him over. I can fix a nice quiche and we can discuss Nixon."

"That would be wonderful," Albert said flatly, too upset to argue.

"It could mean a promotion for you," she continued, passing the champagne once more. "As I was saying to your father—

Albert choked again on the sweet liquid and struggled for breath.

"Have you seen a doctor about that?" Sabrina asked.

"Aunt Sabrina," Albert said, fighting for control, "my father is dead."

"Oh, don't tell him that. He'd be very upset."

"When I was a baby. The train wreck. Don't you remember?"

"Of course, I remember. It was while your father was working on that irrigation project in India, although I don't know why he took that job. Neither he nor your mother knew a word of any of the languages spoken there. What a tragedy. Your poor mother and little Tony dead, and you and your father in the hospital. Why, it was months before you could be brought back to the United States."

"It was my father and my brother who died." Albert tried to say it calmly to keep it straight in his own mind. "_Mother_ and I were in the hospital. Mother is alive and Father is dead."

"Nonsense, I am your mother's mother's sister, I should know if she is dead or alive." She put a thoughtful finger to her chin, "Or am I your father's mother's sister? Let me see, my last name is Alabaster, but that used to be my first name— Well, anyway, I am your great aunt and I know who died. It was your poor mother and your poor twin brother Anthony with that sweet little birthmark on the inside of his thigh. In fact," she added with a delicate hand to her cheek, "if it weren't for that birthmark, we never would have known which twin died and which twin survived.

"Hello, Mom?"

"Albert, what are you calling for?"

"I have to move back home, Mom. I can't take it here. Weird things are happening. This guy keeps calling and threatening to make me eat a Buick, an old man in a toga pops in and out through locked doors. Everyone knows who I am but me. The kitchen is half green. Aunt Frederica isn't Aunt Frederica anymore, she's Aunt Sabrina, and she says that you're dea—"

"Albert, you promised!" There was panic in his mother's voice. "You said you wouldn't move home again."

"This is an emergency," Albert insisted. "I'm going crazy here."

"It's always an emergency. Since you first moved out when you were twenty-four, your whole life has been an emergency." Gathering her courage and holding an image before her of endless nights of Albert dragging her off to monster movies because he was too afraid to go by himself, she firmly said, "Albert, I have my own life and you have yours. Now go out and live it, away from me." Even talking to him reminded her of the smell of stale popcorn.

"But, Mom—"

"I'm kicking you out of the nest, Albert. Goodbye."

Soon after that she moved away from Tacoma declaring, "I've seen my last of Godzilla," and leaving no forwarding address.

"I've discovered your present bewildering situation is directly related to a clogged cog," Faddle told Albert.

"Clogged cog," Albert repeated.

"What else can you expect when you let your life drift through the cosmic machinery?" Faddle said. "It's your own fault by default, Albert."

"Clogged cosmic cog," Albert said. It sounded like one of the tongue twisters he recited in voice and diction class when he was studying to be a radio announcer.

They were sitting in the living room. Albert had just finished vacuuming and dusting the place when Faddle popped in, literally. The kitchen was still just as he had left it the night before, green and yellow and full of paint fumes. The rest of the house had a musty odor, as if it had been raining inside.

"How do you know about the, uhm, the cog?" Albert asked. Two visits from Faddle in one day, Albert was trying to be as calm and mature about it as he could. Since it was all right to humor crazy Aunt Sabrina, Albert decided that it couldn't hurt to humor himself.

"I'm one of the Ancients," Faddle said casually. "We

created THE Universe."

"Wow," Albert said, wondering how impressed he should be with his own imagination. "You created this whole universe."

Faddle rolled his eyes in exasperation, "Not this universe, THE Universe," as if that were a complete explanation.

"Isn't this THE Universe?"

Faddle gave a cackling little laugh then got a faraway look in his eyes, as if remembering the good old days. "Ah, creation! That part is easy. What to do with the garbage, that's the problem. We really should have put more thought into it. This," Faddle spread his arms to encompass the world, "happened by itself out of the coffee grounds, orange rinds, and other remnants swept out after breakfast in THE Universe."

Albert remembered the first flat map of the Earth he had ever seen and how a teacher had explained that it was like the skin of an orange flattened out. After that he kept trying to peel his oranges so the pitted rind would come off in the same shape as the map. He only succeeded in making his mother frantic over his sudden craving for citrus. A vitamin C tablet started showing up by his bowl of cereal every morning.

Motherly concern is certainly short-lived, Albert thought.

To get his mind off of parental abandonment, he tried to recall a poem about an orange. How did it go?

"A few trillion years later," Faddle continued, "we did a little remodeling, came back with another load of refuse and found you here."

"What?" Albert asked as intelligently as he could.

"Not you personally—this universe, the Milky Way, Earth. Since we aren't really sure what we have here, and since we have an instinctive compulsion for bureaucracy, we set up some foundations to study the situation. There's the Foundation for the Research of Almost-Civilized Species, which studies Dolphins, Porpoises, Whales, Granite, and the like."

"Granite?" Albert's mind conjured up an image of the Buick beast in stone. What if he called again?

"Believe me, there was a lot of controversy over that one," Faddle explained, "what with their past barbarism, all that molten activity and their intrusive nature. The decision to include them in the almost-civilized category was based entirely on their more recent solidified social structure and the pedantic works of their philosophers. Great thinkers, the Granite. Wouldn't want to share a pod with one though," he added under his breath.

"And there's the Foundation for the Research of Semi-Civilized Species, which, among other creatures, studies human beings."

"And you like your work?" Albert asked, not really interested in the answer. It was difficult to show enthusiasm for someone else's job when he didn't have one of his own.

"Not at all," Faddle answered flatly.

"If you're this big, terrific Ancient who created THE Universe and all that, then why don't you use a little pull to get another job?"

"If I had any pull," Faddle responded, annoyed, "would I be with the Sanitation Department? But let's get to your cog problem, Albert," he said, changing the subject. "I think I can help you if you'll just keep your sarcastic remarks to yourself and answer a few questions. Now about this train wreck."

Albert hung his head and covered his face with his hands.

"Oh, Aunt Sabrina, I'm going crazy—stark, raving mad. And I don't know what to do about it. I don't know where to get help."

"Believe me, Albert, if anyone knows about being crazy, it's your Aunt Sabrina," she said confidently. "Now, you need two things." With small, delicate steps she slowly traveled from the gold brocade settee where Albert slouched to an antique roll-top desk with carved pillars on each side and cupid faces grinning from the top of each column. The long silk kimono she wore gave her the appearance of floating. Thick black hair piled high on her head held an arrangement of wind chimes that tipped precariously as she walked, sending out a cascade of tinkling off-key music.

"First of all, you mustn't use the word crazy." She rummaged through the rows of pigeonholes while Albert tried to remember what color her hair had been yesterday. "You must say eccentric. Now, where is that letter? Ah, yes, here it is." She handed him the stiff stationery, a piece of limp paper and a stubby pencil. "Now write down that name and address."

"This is a law firm," Albert said confused, but then he was always confused in the presence of his aunt, and since arriving in Minneapolis two days ago, at all other times as well.

"Exactly!" Sabrina raised an index finger into the air triumphantly as if the reason was self-evident. "For the other item—. You're not writing, Albert," she scolded.

"Sorry." He dutifully copied the information printed across the top of the letter.

"Where was I? Oh, yes, the million dollars."

Albert stared up at his aunt, his mouth uselessly hanging open.

"Why, I'll just call up the bank and have the money transferred to your account. They're so wonderful there. They'll take care of everything and then you can stop worrying."

"I don't have a bank account," Albert insisted. "Probably because I don't have any money to put into a bank account." Nervously he started pacing across the thick oriental carpet, paper and pencil still in hand.

"Of course you do, it's at the same bank I use." Albert tried to continue the protest, but Sabrina was already on the phone. "Hello, dear, this is Sabrina Alabaster—Albert, do be quiet—No, dear, not you. I was just speaking to my nephew. Of course, Albert, he's the only living nephew I have, you know. No, he hasn't been sick—you haven't been sick, have you?—just out of town for a little while. Now he's back. I'll be sure to give him your message when I hang up, but right now I need to speak to someone. I think a vice-president will do, or the president if he's available. Yes, thank you, dear. I'm on hold, Albert, now what was it you were rudely trying to say while I was— Oh, hello, Mr. Gabriel, Sabrina Alabaster here. I'd like to give my nephew Albert a million dollars."

Grasping the back of a chair, Albert tried not to faint. Unfortunately, he had grabbed the cane rocking chair. As it tilted backward, Albert fell to the floor with a dull thud. When he came to, his aunt was bending over him with a glass of water. She dipped her finger tips into the liquid then flicked them at him, sending the droplets flying in all directions.

"Here, drink this," she shoved the glass into his trembling hand.

"Thank you, Aunt Sabrina." He looked at the water but didn't drink.

"It's all arranged. Tomorrow morning you can drive me to

the bank and I'll sign the papers. I almost forgot, the young lady on the phone wanted me to tell you that she's missed seeing you at the bank lately. She was most concerned about your health. Tell me, dear, have you made a conquest?"

Albert was glad he was still on the floor; it saved him the trouble of falling again. "I've never set foot in that bank, never, whatever bank it is," he said on the brink of hysteria.

Sabrina stood over him, a knowing look on her powdered face. "You came to me just in time." She pulled him to his feet. For her small, wispy appearance she was actually quite strong. From under the chair where it had landed, she scooped up the paper on which Albert had scrawled the lawyer's address. She folded it and tucked it into Albert's shirt pocket. Then she steered him to the entryway, past the grandfather clock and toward the door. Albert went without protest.

"You'll be fine, Albert dear. You now possess the two things that change you from a crazy person into an eccentric—a million dollars and the name of a good lawyer." She gave him a final shove out the door and into the world.

Albert lugged the stone birdbath bowl a few more steps then stopped to catch his breath. He was glad it had come off of the matching stone pedestal so easily because he wasn't sure he could have lifted them together. If he had taken the time to plan this better, he would have borrowed his aunt's Mercedes when he took her home after their nerve-racking, for Albert anyway, trip to the bank. Instead of having to carry the birdbath, he could have driven it in style to the bridge.

Albert hefted the rough, massive bowl to get a better grip. At least he felt he was doing something himself this time instead of relying on someone else. He couldn't go on living with the hallucinations, and he couldn't stand to be locked up in a white-walled looney bin. If he was some kind of schizophrenic-split personality-manic depressive, which he was convinced he was, then there was only one answer.

He reached the middle of the Hennepin Avenue bridge totally exhausted. He slumped to the sidewalk and sat with the birdbath bowl in his lap. Looking over his shoulder, he could see the brown water of the Mississippi River flowing peacefully under him. Before him cars whizzed past with a whining sound. Albert coughed pathetically as a puff of exhaust fumes engulfed him. A jogger in a sweat suit and head phones stopped, pulled a neatly folded dollar out of his sock, and dropped it into the basin with a crooked, slightly apologetic smile at Albert. Then he set off again to the beat of some private tune.

A few days ago Albert would have been overjoyed at an easy buck. Money had been his biggest worry after losing his job. But now he had a million dollars in a bank he'd never been in before today, where everyone knew him by name. The receptionist asked why he hadn't called her for a date lately, and one of the cashiers hinted that she would love to go to Tahiti with him the next time he went. The next time he went! He'd like to go to Tahiti just once. That was out of the question now, of course, Albert reminded himself, struggling to his feet.

Clutching the birdbath, he swung one leg over the railing, then the other. For a moment he balanced on the thin metal strip, legs in the air, arms hugging the bowl. He teetered backward and forward unable to push himself off, afraid he would fall the wrong direction and be crushed by a stone instead of drowned.

At the next swing forward Albert shoved toward mid-air. He and the vessel plunged dizzily downward and into cold water. Happily Albert clasped the bowl to his chest and sank rapidly to a comfortable crossed-legged sitting position on the silt and weed covered river bottom. He was there for only a few moments when he heard the voice.

"Does this have some social significance?" The bubbles tumbled out of Faddle's mouth and up toward the surface, except for one that caught in his beard and a few that tangled in his buoyant hair.

Albert wondered if he was dead yet. He certainly hoped not, because if he was, then he was just as crazy dead as he was alive.

"I said, is this part of a social ritual?" Again the bubbles. Where did Faddle get the air to keep making all of them?

"It's called suicide," Albert tried to yell, but the words came out in soft round sounds. Round like the bubbles. The cool water wrapped him like a blanket. "And it's done alone so get lost." Ohh, oxygen starvation. "Scram." Carbon dioxide euphoria. "Take a hike." Brain death. "A long walk off a short bridge." Albert laughed uncontrollably at his little joke, not bothering to wonder where he got air to make all the bubbles, bubbles, bubbles. And he suddenly remembered the poem.

> *I dreamt I*
> *was an orange*
> *rind thrown*
> *overboard*
> *floating between—*

Floating between what? Albert wondered what he would float between if he were an orange rind.

"You're not crazy, Albert," Faddle said, trying to keep his long skirt from bobbing up over his face.

"I see you, don't I? That's proof enough for me." One curious little perch swam merrily in and out of the air globs.

"I've got the answers, Albert. All you have to do is ask the questions."

"Oh, yeah? Riddle me this, Batman, how come I'm not dead yet?"

"Because you're wearing a shield," Faddle said. I put it on you. You don't think I let my employees run around on this barbarous planet without protection, do you? You just get one broken in and 'zap' you have to train in another one. I don't have that much time to spend going to funerals."

"You mean I can't die?"

"You can't even cut yourself shaving."

Albert looked around at the numbing, murky water; the strands of weeds swaying with the current; rusty beer cans; the single perch hovering a few feet from his nose. "You're sure?" he asked. Faddle nodded, his hair fanning out around his face like an albino peacock tail. Albert shrugged and let go of the birdbath bowl.

"A lot of people were injured in the train wreck in India," Faddle explained as they slowly walking along Marshall Street, heading toward the house. Albert dripped a dark trail of river water onto the sidewalk. He flapped his arms against his body and rubbed his hands together in an effort to warm up, but he couldn't stop his teeth from chattering. Beside him Faddle was miraculously dry and seemed perfectly comfortable in the sunny spring weather. "They were sent to many different hospitals, some of them miles away from the accident. Apparently, you and your mother were sent to one hospital; your father and brother were taken to another. The record keeping was very untidy," Faddle said with disgust. "As a result, each pair was told that the other pair was dead."

"But how can my brother Anthony be called Albert too? I'm Albert," Albert insisted. "I'm the twin with the birthmark."

"Your father must have thought Albert was the twin without the birthmark; while your mother thought Albert was the twin with the birthmark. I've checked the birth certificates. Neither one mentions a birthmark."

"So I really don't know who I am," Albert said thoughtfully. "For some reason that isn't as upsetting as I think it should be." He twisted a dribble of water out of the pocket of his jacket. He wasn't sure how much he believed the story Faddle had just told him. Improbable as it was, however, it was the only explanation he had; and it did make a certain amount of sense if he didn't think about it too hard. He wondered what his mother would say when he told her his father and brother were still alive. "What happens when the other Albert, my brother, shows up?"

"You may have figured out that he's not very reliable," Faddle complained. "Maybe he won't show up at all. You do want his job as Native Cultural slash Social Historian for the Sanitation Department's Foundation for the Research of Semi-Civilized Species, don't you?"

"I guess I do," Albert said. "I need the job. I just write down what I see people doing?"

"That's it."

"Faddle, wouldn't it be better if you had an expert doing this? I mean, I'm in the middle of all this life stuff. I don't know if I can record it right, objectively and all that," Albert said.

"If we wanted objective," Faddle said sharply, "we would have hired a Granite. The only really meaningful observations are done by those on the front lines."

"That's where I feel like I am," Albert replied.

Faddle gave him a tired, bureaucratic look. "It will give you something to do while I work on that clogged cog. Just don't forget to complete your reports on time."

DANITH McPHERSON

56

Pleiades

Brothers scatter;
but boldly
in Taurus
sisters cluster
across the light years,
lanterned daughters blazing
behind,
before,
together,
ancient torches
incubating
fresh-born fire.

58

Litany for Lost Heroes

The odor of burnt alien flesh pricked my nostrils like crushed peppercorns. The face on the body stretched out on the gurney in front of me had been flamed off, charring away the gravely, reptilian-like skin. Thick liquid oozed over what remained.

Only a week ago the hospital's emergency room had been mostly human casualties. The clientele had shifted now. Our military scientists have learned how to ignite the enemy's tough hide and propel shrapnel through it, deep into tender organs. Gruesomely effective, the new incendiary our ground troops wielded gave us a temporary edge in a war to keep the planet Opal for ourselves—a war we had been losing and still might not be able to win. It had also increased the case load for me and the other ligium-miners-turned-medics to the point of exhaustion.

The ER was madness. I could name each dragon I'd been via my linked connections, but I didn't know how many shifts had passed. Time and what I did within its framework seemed separated from one another.

"Run through your prep, Anna," Dr. Shannon, the leader of the surgical team, told me. As if I needed prompting. Tall, broad and round-faced, she was as arrogant and inclined to delusions of godhood as the rest of the doctors. Unlike most of them, she was willing to repair the invaders. Invaders. The word was frequently used in the media. It cleverly cast humans in the role of innocent victims. Maybe once we had been innocent, back on Earth or wherever we came from before that. But victims? Never. It's not in our nature.

Work on dragons was done in make-shift spaces adjoining the ER. The real operating rooms were reserved for human patients, even when they sat empty. I locked a coupler into the receptor that had been implanted in the creature's skull moments ago when it had been admitted to the hospital. Usually the linking hardware was embedded in the forehead, but this one didn't have enough of it left. The wire and plastic circle had been placed in the crown instead. According to the surgeons, a dragon didn't have specialized areas of the brain, so any entry point would serve. We miners knew that wasn't true.

I ran a hand along the attached cable, feeling for imperfections in the delicate filaments, especially where the bundle split into twin serpents. The glass threads felt clean, ready for me to link with the dragon—an absurdly mythical title but more flattering than the other terms applied to the beings.

The usual conversations flowed around me like water avoiding a rock. "The dragons are worried about their MIAs." Shannon spoke to her surgical crew, which didn't include me. I labored with them for hours, for days, at a time; but I was not one of them. In their minds I was as non-human as the dragons.

Shannon found ways to remind me of the division. At regular intervals she reported me to the conduct board for refusing to shave my head in compliance with regulations. She knew I never got more than a reprimand and another notation added to my lengthy list of infractions. With a mere twenty-four miners stationed at this facility, no one was going to kick me out for having bristly black spikes barely longer than eyelashes. Scarcely a meter and a half tall, I have the gaunt, ghostliness common to all miners. My dark hair and amber skin show my Earth-Asian ancestry, and my blue eyes reveal that I can trace my lineage back to the original Helsinki Settlement. I'd routinely broken more sacred regulations than the skinhead one.

The shriek of an approaching siren was standard white noise. I concentrated on the diagnostic lights flashing across the interface in my forearms. Designed for piloting a mole pod, since the war, the hardware had been modified for this grislier purpose. The display was mesmerizing. I lost myself in the pattern and slipped into a fatigue-induced waking-sleep. A scream of pain from the next cubical jerked me back from what we miners called mental treading. It was like being caught head-on in a slush stream. Snug inside the pod, you're encased in your own little world with your treads spinning, unable to move forward. That was me, for a long time now, treading.

"A citizens group," Shannon said to her team. "Imagine that, a lizard citizens group. They want us to give them the hospital records, so they can figure out which of their soldiers ended up here."

I cringed at Shannon's use of the popular derogatory term. Lizards. That's what we miners were called when people wanted to negate the dangerous work that we did—-that we used to do. Lizards, after the poisonous, thick-skinned creatures that ruled the frozen tundra.

Although Shannon had not been addressing me, I said, "Isn't that what we'd ask of them if the positions were reversed and we had no POWs to trade for our own? Wouldn't we at least want to find out what had happened to the soldiers we'd lost?"

I knew the dragons' pleas would be ignored. Each enemy body, whether injured or dead, was a bargaining chip. Our military collected them while theirs didn't. We miners speculated that perhaps the dragons had no place to keep humans in their land camps on Opal and no suitable facilities for them on their orbiting ship. They probably didn't have a clue how to repair us—we certainly struggled to patch up their unfamiliar anatomy. Or maybe they simply had little experience with warfare and no concept of prisoners. It seemed we miners were the only ones with that opinion.

During the last lull in the fighting, as the twenty-four of us had huddled together in the dingy staff room, awaiting the next wave of casualties, Yuri had said we couldn't be expected to think the way regular people did. Yuri. My wonderful Yuri. As fair as I am dark, his eyes as blue as mine.

"Maybe it's because of our physical mods. And our experiences." He'd paused. "And the ore." He had tried to make it remote, as if these things belonged to other people and not to us. But they were embedded in our flesh and entwined in our brains.

We had all been quiet then. The miners from the other five teams had slowly slipped away like shadows until it had been only Team Pi—Yuri, Nikos, Katia and me—left staring at the walls of painted cinderblock. This was not a modern structure of ligium metal but an old concrete complex that drained the life from us. Ligium was too expensive for this, the poorest of the medical facilities. Only aliens and unlucky humans ended up here.

Yuri was right and he was wrong. We had been changed by our profession; but even before being recruited by LitGo, we were light years away from being regular people. Isn't that why the company had come looking for us? We had the small statures and the giant appetites for adventure of the original crazies who had charged off to Opal and made it a colony. We were throwbacks, adrenaline junkies in a terminally civilized world. My parents had repeatedly told me the highly structured, overly regulated societies that dwelled in the warm equatorial band girdling the planet could not be expected to tolerate my unruly behavior. I was sure to end up in prison or under supervised sedation. They hadn't said it in exactly those words, but that's what they'd meant.

When the LitGo recruiter, waiting for me outside the courthouse after having paid fines for my latest crime against the people, had put a contract in front of me, I'd slapped my thumb against the appropriate square without hesitation. Being a miner gave me everything I had lusted for—danger, excitement, and an outrageous salary. With all that on my side, I thought I could handle the general population's revulsion at my job-required, implanted electronics. I never imagined I'd end up here, staring at a faceless alien on the gurney before me.

"I bet there isn't any citizens group," an orderly said. "It's probably just propaganda."

"Stupid lizards." The head nurse didn't even give me an apologetic glance. "They must have weapons on their ship. Why don't they just sit up there and blast us instead of sending ground troops?"

"Sure," I said, "that's what we'd do if we were the ones in orbit. We'd probably end up melting down the two-thirds of Opal that's ice and snow and flooding all of the inhabitable land, but we would've won." They ignored me with a tense silence, as they always did when I tried to be part of the conversation. "Besides," I couldn't stop myself from blurting out, "maybe they have a right to be here."

Despite the crowding and chaos, it seemed as if every decibel of sound—clink of instruments, murmurs, moans— was suddenly sucked away. After several eternal seconds Shannon pierced the vacuum. "When you're done with your shift, you'll report for a psych eval."

Another one? I might. I might not. As the war stretched on and on, the psychs had gotten so stingy with the drugs.

I plugged the snake heads into my wrists, linking myself to the dragon. The emergency room receded. Pain invaded part of my brain. The rest of my mind tried to convince me the suffering didn't belong to me. A chem patch under the short sleeve of my medical greens kept me from panic and shock, but my body still trembled.

I heard Shannon's voice as if it came from some other world. "Talk to me, Anna."

I described the tissue, nerve and organ damage, as I had learned to do more from experience than training. As long as the dragon and I were connected, it was my body, too. Shannon cut away blackened hide. I guided her to the scattered shrapnel. She repaired what she could see and what I could tell her. There were few diagnostic machines that worked on the aliens. The military had no plans to tap strained resources to develop more. It had been easier to adapt the existing neural links used to hardwire miners to their pods, simpler to turn us into human interpreters of alien flesh. At first we did it because the war had taken away the mining and we were bound up in contracts. Then it became something else.

Opal appeared to be coming out of an ice age when the first human colonists arrived. Massive frozen sheets were pulling back toward the poles like a split nut shell, allowing the emergence of a green equatorial swath that must have sparkled like a promising emerald to my ancestors. The planet's abundant natural resources fit beautifully into their paradigm of energy, and some of the existing plant life was easily modified for agricultural purposes.

Unfortunately, the vats of organic building material they'd hauled across space were destroyed in an accident during landfall. They spent several difficult generations experimenting with native substitutes until they discovered an ore scraped from the mountains to the north and left behind by shrinking glaciers. Ligium. They learned to transform it into a usable metal, and so civilization moved forward and upward into layered cities. Of course, the few tons that could be easily collected at the border with the still icy region were inadequate for a growing society. The mining profession, my chosen career, was born from an increasing dependence on the rock.

When the war started, over a thousand teams, working out of three hundred plus mobile refineries, occupied the northern expanse so thick with snow that it had smoothed the mountains and valleys into vast plains broken only by the occasional jagged pyramid of rock, its base a league or more below the surface. Plugged into the controls of our mole pods, we dove into the frozen pockets, seeking deposits of the valuable ore. We chewed it up like beasts, then returned to refineries to excrete it from our bowels. We kept the cities growing, while the people who lived in them shunned us.

The dragons' first assaults had been on the refineries. The rest of the world wondered why, but we miners knew.

Hot furnaces and belching smokestacks had exploded like Landing Day fireworks, incinerating the pods and personnel in a flash. The moles out in the field had returned fat with ore to find the wreckage of their homes sunk into quickly freezing lakes of melted snow. Stranded, they sat waiting for help. When their batteries were finally exhausted and the cold seeped in, the machines and their integrated drivers died. The company and the government, in a rush to protect the remaining refineries, had never sent rescue parties. It had never even occurred to them.

Ironic. Through their initial acts of war, the dragons had ended up hurting themselves. The surviving miners had become their surrogates in the operating room. We were the saviors of the enemy; therefore, traitors to our own kind. No one understood what we'd lost. No one acknowledged that we'd been forced into the role. The company practically owned us. They had the legal right to modify our wiring and reassign us. Maybe they even gleaned enough profit to replace the interrupted ligium sales.

We were good at what we did. The best traitors possible. That made us the targets of suspicious looks and barbed comments. We were MILs, Missing In Life, whether on the tundra or in the operating room.

While Shannon and her crew sliced and diced, I let myself flow into that part of the dragon's mind that we miners had discovered. The patient felt no pain there. It seemed to be a defense mechanism, a retreat into memories.

Tell me your name, I communicated without language. Show me your face. From the beginning we miners collected the identities of our dragons. I knew the name and image of each one I'd linked with. In my dreams I saw their pebbly triangular faces set with large, copper eyes.

My current dragon floated through a montage. It thought of many names and showed me many faces, none its own. Spouses, children, relatives, friends, not friends. There were children and happy expressions, one special child.

Name, I demanded.

It withdrew from my intensity. I gave it a vision, a vista of a city with soaring spiraled steeples preserved under a canopy of milky glass. It seemed comforted.

I tried again, softer. I saw a reflection that matched what the dragon's features must have looked like before they'd been ripped and charred. The face felt like mine. It was a good face. The dragon thought about itself. He thought about himself. He was a male, according to the physiology our doctors have decided to call male. Together we knew tragedy, boredom and joy. There were people close to me in a room of many colors that I wandered in for hours, absorbing the fragrance of blooming plants. This was more real than any life I'd ever had on my own. But I still didn't have an answer.

You, I urged silently. An outside voice tried to pull me away. A tightening panic spread through my nerves. I insisted. You.

The connection snapped. I tumbled back to ER.

"We're finished with this one, Anna," Shannon said sternly.

A nurse stood staring at me as if I were a freak, a dangling cable in his hand. Shannon must have been shrieking at me for some time and finally had him pull the plug. The dragon, receptor in his head now empty, was on his own. And so was I. I felt violated and severed from myself.

"You're done for the day," Shannon commanded. She efficiently went on to the next task. "Orderly, find me another lizard and get the next dragon in here stat."

Wearily, I walked through the chaos, only marginally aware that I had just served a triple shift. Yuri, Katia and Nikos, as worn out as I was, were waiting for me in the passage to the underground barracks we shared. The military was beyond frustration with our refusal to be split up into separate quarters and had ceased trying to force us. Voracious sexual needs were part of the miner myth. Commanding officers probably worried that we would explode into a raping rampage if we didn't have our own orgies every night. Sometimes myths are useful.

We dragged ourselves through the tunnel. I put an arm around Yuri's waist. We'd all grown thin. Away from the ice and the ore, there was no pleasure in food. Yuri's pale, curly hair was darkened by sweat. The other surgeons lacked Shannon's preoccupation with the bald rule and, I think, were afraid of us.

Katia kept a fingertip against the concrete wall as she shuffled forward. We were so tired that we might have wandered off in the wrong direction if we'd had anything but a straight passage before us. "Nine hours on one dragon." Her head was shaved expect for a blazing orange braid dangling from the crown to her knees. Despite all we'd been through, her oval face was still sweet and her gold-flecked eyes were serene.

Nikos gave me a faint smile in greeting. Skin as pale as dust and eyes so deeply brown you could sink into them and never want to come out, he shaved his head by choice. An array of chem patches was plastered across his neck. I wondered how he had stolen so many and how he managed even a wobbly walk with such a large quantity of drugs soaking into his skin. He put a hand on Katia's shoulder to steady himself. "I miss the ride," he murmured.

A sudden craving gripped my chest. The day before the war engulfed me again like a cocoon. I couldn't pull in a breath. Yuri grabbed me by the shoulders and slammed me against the wall until I inhaled. Nikos was tired and drugged and probably didn't realize he'd spoken out loud; so later, much later, I might forgive him for reminding me of my own weakness.

There are no retired miners. Officially, deaths were attributed to malfunctioning pods; to avalanches that turned the little moles into coffins; or to pilots becoming disoriented in the featureless terrain, unable to find their way back to the refinery before their power ran out. Those things happened, but they were usually only fatal because the miner had gotten entangled in the seductive influence of the rock. In the ecstasy of the ride.

Exposure to the raw ore altered the brain. We felt it. We lived it. We slowly became addicted to it.

The government and LitGo—really, how different were they from one another—guarded that secret for fear the populace would abandon the metal cities. They professed that the processed ligium was safe. Maybe it was true. Maybe not. As we miners had discovered, they weren't very good at full disclosure.

In the dim underground light all I wanted was to be wired into the mole pod again, following the ore song that resonated through the frozen world. Yuri guided me back to the concrete bunker that served as home.

Katia had developed into a gifted artist and had covered the coarse walls with beaded cords. I closed my eyes and listen to their subtle chiming. That night I slept hard. When I woke the next morning, tremors plagued my fingers. They crept through my implants into my arms and body. I curled up into a quivering ball on my bunk. Yuri sat with me in case I stopped breathing. Distantly I heard Katia say she'd report the two of us as sick.

When we were alone, I knew Yuri wanted to whisper of his own craving for the ore. It was often on his lips when he kissed me. I trusted him to stay silent. He got me through the sunless hours in our subterranean barracks. I was stable by the time Katia and Nikos returned. Nikos brought me surgical gloves inflated with helium and decorated with silly faces to show his contrition.

The next day Yuri and I returned to work. A week of double shifts and wild rumors followed. When the cease fire hit, we appreciated the break but were soon bored by inactivity. While dignitaries sat in luxury hotel rooms discussing the MIA issue, we were stuck within gray walls with nothing purposeful to do. That was always a dangerous circumstance for us. I wondered how the two sets of aliens had solved the language barrier.

Our single room was small and feeling smaller with every inactive day and new rumor. Katia juggled scalpels she'd appropriated, despite the tight security and the close watch the hospital cops kept on us. I lit matches and flicked them at Yuri. He snatched them from the air with thumb and forefinger then extinguished the flames by rolling them on his tongue. Gotta' love those enhanced reflexes. None of the speculations said the hospital was preparing to surrender records on its dragon patients. Knowledge was power. The government wasn't likely to toss a single free crumb across the table.

The demand for information on MIAs became an obsession with us. With me. During those idle days we modified snake heads and linked into the hospital's digital network. When wounded dragons were admitted, the hospital slapped a number on each one and made a vidgraph. We twenty-four former miners navigated the data as if still searching for ore. We found our dragons and transferred their images to portable devices. Most of the angular faces in the illegally accessed records had hideous wounds that conflicted with our mental portraits that had come from the dragons themselves. In our minds they were not the broken captives in the vids but whole, undamaged beings.

I'd found the record that matched the nameless dragon I carried with me. When it appeared on the screen, burnt and faceless, my eyes snapped shut and wouldn't open. Katia copied it to my viewer for me then blanked the screen. She touched my hand to let me know it was safe to look.

We learned which of our dragons had succumbed to their wounds, and we mourned each one. We discovered which ones had survived, but we couldn't find out where they were. The final entry on each hospital record was the same. RMC. Released into military custody. We wormed our way into Central Command but could not pick up the thread.

Yuri developed a nasty twitch in his left eye. Katia frantically filled sheet after sheet with drawings. They spilled off the paper onto the cold floor, creating a charcoal mosaic of dragon faces. We were kicked out of our barracks by armed guards. When we were allowed back in, the faces were gone, as if they had no right to be visible. The walls were stripped of the hanging beads.

Nikos pressed his palms against the rough, bare bricks. "With the cease fire, at least it gave the soldiers something to do."

We considered transmitting the raw records we'd gathered to the dragon ship but discarded the idea. Even if their version of technology could decipher human code, how could we coldly send them such monstrous images? How could we explain who was dead and who might still be alive? Our intent was sure to be misinterpreted.

I flicked another flaming match at Yuri. "If only we could give them something of what they've lost. We have to find a way to deliver what we know." For me there was also the problem of the patient whose name I didn't have, the one so damaged he could never be identified by his hospital vid. He had died but he was always with me, cradled next to the hollow absence of ore.

Nikos, pale and broodingly handsome, hung by his knees from a trapeze he'd bolted to the ceiling, arms folded across his chest like an inverted god. "We know a lot about being lost but not much about deliverance."

A new rumor rumbled through the idle staff like low thunder. The government was using the lull to put the finishing touches on a fleet of spacecraft that could shoot down the orbiting alien ship and the smaller craft that delivered dragon troops to the ground.

Yuri linked with Central Command and found out the fleet was real. "Designed for wired pilots, just like the pods."

Katia examined the covertly obtained technical drawings. "You move in three dimensions. Snow or space, no difference. With a little study any of us could do it."

Yuri forced a grin. "But it won't be us. They've already modified new recruits."

Nikos swung upside down.   It had become his usual position. "They don't trust us."

"It's practically an invitation," Katia said. We were still seething about the desecration of her beautiful artwork. They thought they could obliterate anything that didn't fit their official doctrine. "We should pull an Unauthorized Use, just to show them they can't ignore their own creations."

Unauthorized Use, a euphemism for theft. I gulped for air. To take the ride again. Any kind of ride. Yuri wrapped himself around me until I could manage regular breaths.

The next day the twenty other miners came to our barracks and we laid out a plan. There was no reason to wait. Yuri spoofed a high-ranker and issued fraudulent orders. Far away at Garvey Airfield, personnel scrambled, preparing for a secret test flight of one of the newly developed craft. The motor pool dispatched a truck to rendezvous with the elite pilots and technicians—identities undisclosed, and this event was not happening—in a secluded area. Hospital security never knew we left the compound.

Our escorts, slick with perspiration, gave us furtive glances, trying covertly to see our faces under the hoods of ponchos mottled with camouflage colors. The moment we arrived at the air field, we were ushered like VIPs to a midnight-black sphere set on shiny prongs, like a dark gem mounted in a silver ring. We knew by the way the light melted into the surface, by the way it sang to us, that it was made of ligium. Our ore, perhaps the last we had extracted.

The metallic bubble was cramped with all of us sharing an environment designed for a normal crew of eight. Yuri held me through the quaking launch and kept a hand to my chest to monitor my breathing.

Katia had tweaked Nikos' implants to make them

compatible with the craft's controls. His launch wouldn't have gotten him many points, but his navigation scored big time in style.

The dragon ship wasn't hard to find. Not sure how to approach an alien enemy, we flew straight to the front door and knocked. I think that convinced the startled occupants— along with the diminutive size of our vehicle in comparison to theirs—that it was not an attack, although it took them several agonizing hours to be certain.

The dragon ship swallowed the capsule, and we came to rest in what looked like a cargo bay. We left the sphere slowly, in ones and twos, to show we were not an army. Muscular dragons, who seemed to be guards, formed a menacing reception line between us and a crowd that trailed out a wide door. One of the guards jabbered at us in incomprehensible syllables that didn't sound like warm greetings. Nikos offered it the oval box of his portable viewer in explanation for our visit. A dragon snatched it from his hand as if it were a weapon. I pressed my own to my chest, afraid it would be taken from me.

For all the beings crammed into the large space, it was deathly quiet. Katia unfolded a piece of paper. The crackle seemed to charge the air. She held out a charcoal drawing she'd made of one of her patients. "Nal-nar." She pronounced the name as best she could.

The dragons muttered among themselves.

"Nal-nar." She spoke louder and raised the paper for those beyond the guards to see. The others held their breaths, while I concentrated on breathing.

A sound that was similar yet enormously different, like a blossom to a bud, echoed from the back. A dragon, shorter and of a slighter build than those who separated us from the gathering, squeezed toward us but was blocked by the sentries. It spoke in a flood of multitones. The guards—so much like our own, no wonder we were at war—scowled with uncertainty and wouldn't budge.

Katia stepped close to one of the living fence posts, the top of her head barely reaching the middle of its chest. She locked it in a stare. So quickly it couldn't stop her, she stretched her arm passed its shoulder, offering the sketch to the arguing dragon. Claws grasped her arm to force it back. She released the paper. The small dragon scooped it up like a falling bird. The parent or sibling or lover examined the charcoal lines then carefully cradled the parchment in its arms. One MIA was no longer missing.

After that we spent most of our time in a large room with a crowd always around us. We were assigned guides who listened to our mispronounced litanies and examined the grotesque vidgraphs on the tiny screens of our viewers. Nikos had us act out scenes that we hoped made them understand that these dragons had been in a place that gave medical care. It was harder, in many ways, to indicate some were dead and some were now being held in POW camps. At least, we thought that's where the survivors were. It was less than satisfying information, but it was all we had to give them.

Once they seemed to understand our initial explanation, we used shortcuts. An open hand meant alive and held captive. A hand to the heart and a bowed head meant death. They were confused by the tears that accompanied both gestures.

It seemed every dragon on the gigantic ship had someone who hadn't come home. Encouraged by Katia's portrait, they arrived clutching images and statues. They shoved them hopefully toward us. The officials soon ordered the unruliness stopped. From then on the spectators sat on the floor or stood quietly at a distance, but they would not leave.

Our guides grimaced at the damaged flesh we showed them. They each had a device that searched visual files of their own soldiers. It was not always easy to match the two versions of the same being. Of the same person.

My helper, more composed than the others, would halt at a 3D image and ask the same question again and again, the same string of sounds that I couldn't translate but that I understood. "This one?" Its wedge-shaped face had a slight fullness to the cheeks. A yellow tinge lightened its pebbly forehead. Patient, expectant, its copper eyes stared at my grotesquely smooth skin. "Is it this one?"

The guide gradually learned the sound equivalents I used to speak the names. It became adept at translating my sour notes into dragon music. As the days passed, the audience dwindled. I watched the spouses and children and relatives and friends and not friends as they drifted away. Relief, worry, hope, grief cycled through each movement, each posture. Had I learned to read dragon expressions or was I projecting my own onto the faces around me? One by one Nikos, Katia, Yuri and the others reached the end of their records and recollections.

I displayed the vid that went with the last name I had, the second to the last dragon that was mine. A twitch in my fingers spread to my hands. My breathing grew jagged. I pronounced it as best I could with my foreign tongue. My guide showed me a visual. I nodded, and held out my open hand, unable to make a sound. The guide announced it to the few remaining. Two dragons sighed, others touched them lightly with sympathy, and perhaps a shade of envy, as they left the room.

The guide saw my deteriorating condition but didn't know how to interpret it.

"One—more," I gasped. Reluctantly I showed it the last image. After stoically enduring so much, it turned away. I didn't have the language to describe the vital, animated features I saw when I closed my eyes. I didn't have the talent to draw it. I didn't have a name. I felt myself slip into a stream of rushing slush. I was treading, trying to move forward but caught in place.

In the month before the war, my growing addiction to the ore had swelled to eclipse everything, even my Yuri. I should have broken my contract and left the company. But I didn't. I couldn't. No one ever had.

On the last day of ordinary insanity, the day before the first attack, I pulled an Unauthorized Use. I stole a pod and drove across a glacier without a thought. All I wanted was the ride.

I didn't need the mole's instruments to tell me where I was headed in the bleached landscape. My blood was guided by the heat of a rich lode, hidden below tons of snow that filled a valley. The tops of the mountains surrounding it stuck out like human-high pyramids.

I killed the exterior lights and plunged into a promising ice wave, too eager to stop and check the stability of the loose shards pressed together, giving the illusion of a solid.

The structure turned fragile from my hasty burrowing. It slid sideways then collapsed under me. An avalanche of frozen slivers propelled the pod down and down through pockets of air and frost, finally slamming it against sweet ore.

I laughed at the sudden flush of intoxication and wanted more. The huge grinning teeth I controlled chewed hungrily and swallowed great lumps. I pounded at my nerves and wires, thrusting deeper into the rock. Ligium, like blood, like my blood, pulsed along the channels to the storage bins around me. My every cell gulped the drug-laced electricity. A river of slush filled the cavity behind me, blocking my exit, but I never considered reverse. I had no desire to escape. I was immersed in the ride. Nothing else had context or meaning.

The bins filled and refused to take more, triggering the grinders to toss the rock aside like waste. I couldn't allow even a speck of precious ore to be cast aside, so I disabled the grinders. The pod groaned to a halt. Building pressure from the ice at my back squeezed the mole against the rock. The walls screeched. Instruments red lined, sending warning spikes through my arms, like burning needles. The sensation of the ore muted the pain. I could have endured a torturer's probe. The grinder's teeth, spread wider than the hull, began to bend at the edges. It curved back against the mole's skin like a comforting hug.

I was joyous and content to implode in my tomb. I would be a fly in white amber, preserved in the heart of a gem, immortal in the soul of a planet.

A lurch snapped me deep into the cushioned couch. The scrape of crystal on metal whined like a collapsing scaffold. Ore shattered free in front of me.

I was spit out, expelled. A gushing subterranean stream swept the pod forward through the core of an ice and rock mountain. Jolted from my coma, I felt bitter cold seep into my failing environment. The current tumbled the mole through a water-carved tunnel. Disoriented, damaged sensors screamed their confusion. I silenced them and listened to the rushing and banging against the hull.

Roaring water became many voices, as if echoing a name,

the word it called itself, over and over. The pod spun. It was shoved and buffeted. It lodged against something solid. Trembling, I opened the irises of the exterior beacons. The ones that still functioned cast uneven beams.

I gazed beyond the cracked view screen in awe.

I was on a frozen plain beside a river of floating pearls. Around me loomed a gigantic cavern, domed above the reach of my lights. It seemed when the ice age descended upon this valley, a bubble had forced it to skim along the tops of peaks, leaving the lowland almost untouched. The frosted ground was smooth in places and cobbled in others, implying pathways. Hollows might once have been rich with plants. Buildings, scalloped with arches, sprouted thick towering spirals. Here, where they had been protected from the brutal weather and the crawling glaciers, they continued to soar like hopes and dreams.

The patterns were unlike those from a human architect but still recognizable as having intent and meaning. To my eyes, some were grotesque, while others were glorious. They were all exquisite. The ligium in them sang to me, and I knew the stories spread among the miners and discounted by the company as ore-induced deliriums were true.

We were not the first here. This was not our planet. We had no right to it. It belonged to the dragons.

I gasped at the beauty as it faded along with the mole's beacons. I gasped the dead air of my failing pod until there was nothing more my lungs could pull from it. Since there was no longer any point to it, I ceased breathing.

When Yuri realized I was missing, he searched the bleak landscape until he discovered the broken wave. He dove after me, surfing the turbulent slush into the cavern. He coupled our pods together and pumped warm air through the emergency duct. Then he dragged my crippled mole from its beautiful grave, across kilometers of snow to the refinery bay. He pried my body, stiff with tremors, from the capsule and held me, knowing I would have preferred to die in the arms of the ore.

Now in the cavern of the alien ship, the vision of my near suicide made the quaking return. One more missing must be found, one more must be pulled from the snow, even if everyone had written her off as unsalvageable.

Yuri rested his hands on my shoulders and spoke so only I could hear. "Anna, I found you. Remember you are found."

The other miners huddled around. Katia gestured at my guide and tapped the device that displayed the files.

The guide showed a new image. Again, Katia indicated. Again. It wrinkled its forehead, perhaps in frustration. The flashing variations of mottled skin and copper eyes became a blur. Yuri shook me to keep me breathing.

A flat picture suddenly imposed itself into the three-dimensional display, a portrait of a dragon composed of layered bits of something like tinted tissue paper. Talons grasped it from the top. I followed the claw and sleeved arm to the face.

The dragon spoke quietly, like water.

I recognized the desperation that knotted the features. I gazed at a mirror of my own tight lips and pleading eyes.

The dragon bore a resemblance to the portrait, but the face behind the hope was unfamiliar to me. And the portrait was of a stranger.

"No." I was unable to repeat the liquid name the dragon had offered.

I felt snow caving in around me and I tasted stale, recycled air. My body trembled. Black spots obscured by vision until the only thing I saw was the lost dragon inside of me.

I'll find you. I forced a slow inhale—exhale—inhale.

I will find you.

DANITH McPHERSON

82

Attic

Life suddenly surprises me
with its clutter.
I can't walk around in it anymore.
I trip over grand ideas and ideals,
stumble across mementos too shiny, too large
to carry in a pocket or hold for very long.
I put one down,
 scrap my shin on its sharp edge.
If only less people strolled in and out.
If only the walls didn't tilt
against my efforts to prop them up
and aligned them with reality.
The frame twists like toothpicks
about to fold,
but there is no room for a collapse
and I could not survive the added mess.
Life is an attic.
Only a block-long yard sale
can save me now,
with poems and
people I used to know
presented for "best offer."

84

Shifting Spirits

Douglas Sandoval woke up dead. Last night he'd curled up in his sleeping bag a whole man and fallen heavily into slumber in this dismal land. Now his loose spirit, no longer tethered to his body, floated above a desert of black soil. The vista shocked him more keenly than his perilous situation. For miles and miles, barren hills caught the rising sun, forming pale slopes leading to empty charcoal valleys. Clots of gray dust whirled into the air with sudden fury then lost interest and drifted back into the monotony.

Minnesota wasn't supposed to look like this. But it did now.

Seeing so much of the devastation at once made it harder to believe. It had been easier to accepted the change a little at a time during the past days trudging through the landscape on solid legs. There should be fir trees heavy with pine cones, squirrels and noisy birds. There should be lakes edged by shy deer. Even though Sandoval knew better, he still held an image of blue and green in his head from—well, he wasn't sure where it came from. Not from personal experience. He'd barely been out of Arizona before this shit-awful, fool's errand, trying to catch a madman.

"Get back—in your—body and—stop messing—around," Raymond Recino, Sandoval's traveling companion, yelled in a panicked cadence from far below.

Sandoval looked straight down and was suddenly gripped by vertigo. A miniature Recino leaned over a sprawled doll-man. He struggled to wrap something neon orange around the figure's chest. "We're not—on vacation—here!"

Sandoval could see the doll's head now. It had a face he saw when he looked in a mirror. Startled by his dual positions, he felt air rush from under him. He plummeted like a boulder toward his physical self. The ground, a layer of arid silt barely covering packed earth, became hard against his spine. Back in his body, he blinked up at Recino. "Sorry. I've been slipping some lately."

"You and your wife." Recino shook shocking orange at him. "You weren't wearing your vest. I can't keep you breathing and get you into this at the same time."

"It's hard to sleep in." He meekly took the overly-bright device and put it on. Doc Rita had invented the thing. She called it a CPR aid. It translated the force from a manual pump into the right amount of pressure.

"Get used to it. It's bad enough I have to spend every night with one eye cocked to make sure you don't turn blue and croak." Recino grabbed a water jug. "I had to give you mouth-to-mouth, man. If I'd had to do compressions by hand, I probably would have bust up your ribs." He took a swig and gargled loudly to show his annoyance. He puckered up as if to spit, thought better of it, and swallowed the precious liquid instead. "Bat-shit breath. You were almost a corpse that time." His slight build shivered. "Never would have touched you then."

Sandoval had trouble feeling grateful to Recino for saving his life. He told himself if he wasn't still dizzy and out of breath, he would get right up and shove his fist against the guy's extremely flat nose for the crack about his wife. He had warned him before, but it only seemed to increase the number of times Recino worked it into the conversation. The thought of Althea, his once steady and faithful Althea, enjoying the touch of another man—of other men—made Sandoval crazy. He wouldn't let himself think about the even wilder rumors and his personal suspicions. He just wouldn't think about them. He just wouldn't.

Yeah, he should slug Recino in that ugly face, pocked and blistered as the fallen tree trunks that poked like bones through the dirt. Instead he felt a compulsion to apologize again for not being able to control his own spirit.

He ached to explain that he didn't hate his wife for what he suspected her of doing, and he very much wanted to defend his coming along on this trip even though he was of no good use. Recino wouldn't want to hear any of it anyway. Sandoval pushed himself onto an elbow and waited for the queasiness to pass. "I saw something when I was—you know."

"Dancing with the wind? Enjoying the view, while I suffered toxic, guano halitosis to keep you alive? I hope it was Narbona." Recino knew he shouldn't be so hard on Sandoval, but being all sympathetic and mushy-hearted wouldn't help either of them get through this. He handed the guy a ration of jerky and dried fruit then passed him the jug. The man was a mess. Anyone could see that by the way he slumped like a beaten dog. What the hell was Old Henry thinking when he practically ordered him to take Sandoval along? As the best tracker, he was the logical one to go after Narbona, but he should have done it alone.

He had no personal interest in Lloyd Narbona. The guy had always been selfish, and he could be mean when crossed. He could go where he pleased as far as Recino was concerned. But then, he might feel differently if was one of the afflicted himself. Doc Rita needed the runaway back, so, okay, he'd go get him.

At the time he thought the task would be a distraction from the staccato of rain, the constant battle against mold and invading vines, and the flooding from new rivers that ran red with clay. Arizona wasn't supposed to be like that. But it was now.

Maybe he hoped going on a tracking expedition would give him something he couldn't find in the strangely mashed up community the place had become. The Doc had left a metro hospital to rescue her parents and had decided to stay. A family of five, who spoke broken English in public and some other language among themselves, knew how to plant in soggy land. A war vet with one leg did paintings that made you weep at the beauty. Everyone brought something important. Even when that something wasn't obvious.

Survival, that's what it was.

Blood still had meaning, but they were now a tribe of survivors and that was to be respected.

Instead of giving Recino a boost, the journey had worn him down. Of course, he hadn't expected it to take so long. Twelve hundred miles, he estimated, Arizona to Minnesota, following the trail of a lunatic.

Sandoval chewed his breakfast. Silence was easier than the simplest conversation with Recino. He felt the medallion Althea had given him, when she still loved him, where it rested lightly against his chest. Maybe it had become a bad marriage, but he still believed in it.

He tried not to think of anything except returning with Narbona so Doc Rita and Old Henry could find a solution to this loose spirit stuff. Recino had no right to give him a hard time about his condition. It's not like he was the only one or like it was his fault. He sure didn't choose to separate from his body, and he definitely couldn't control it. He didn't know what caused it any more than anyone else.

It must be connected to the bizarre-o weather. It would be weird if it wasn't. Weirder, anyway. Human-made climate change or the satellite beams that were supposed to correct it. Take your pick.

The guy from Memphis said he wasn't a scientist but he knew for a fact the magnetic charges on the poles were flipping. The north pole was becoming the south pole, and the south was becoming the north. Sandoval wondered if that meant Santa Claus had to move.

Whatever caused it, eight people Sandoval knew died before they figured out it was happening. With the spirit gone, the heart ceased beating and breathing stopped. Doc Rita trained everyone in CPR. She organized a group to make the vests, using an experimental design her hospital had been working on.

For long rainy days after the deaths, Old Henry was sullen and silent, leaving the rest of the living on their own to deal with a string of funerals and with the "wanderers," as those plagued with roaming spirits were being called. Two more died.

Old Henry finally broke his silence. "Human foolishness has rubbed against the rope that's tied us to this land for centuries. Now it unravels. We are losing our tether to the earth." Thunder from still another storm rolled behind his words, making them sound wise and right.

Sandoval understood what the singer said about as well as he usually did. He wasn't afflicted then, not yet. He already suspected Althea was but kept it to himself. She was spending a lot of her evenings at her sister's, so she said. She came home late, if she came home at all. He didn't ask questions. He told himself he didn't want to hear her lies, but he was really afraid she would tell him the truth.

Old Henry and the other spiritual leaders met and discussed and meditated. Some were officially ordained. Others were self-declared, including a Voodoo priestess from Louisiana who used to sell real estate that was now under water, and a computer coder from Silicon Valley. All ideas were considered. This was a new situation and it required creativity. Narbona volunteered to be the guinea pig for their solution.

The apprentice put items that were important to him into a small metal box. He was tall with muscle-broad shoulders. Sandoval wished he looked like that. Then Althea would be with him every night.

The bits the young man had chosen to represent himself were too personal to display. Sandoval thought he caught a shiny glint and a tuft of something bound in red. The container wasn't very big. He hopped it held more than a bullet from the rifle Narbona kept wrapped in a wolf pelt, and a lock of hair from Althea's younger sister or one of the sad, beautiful girls clustered around the altar—or maybe it was a snip of his own.

Candles, incense and burning herbs filled the room with smoke, while rain and wind clawed at the roof. Chants and songs. Drums, violins and clacking bones. Readings from books and recitals from memory. Sprinkled oils and blood. A dead chicken. An equally dead cell phone. Calling on all the power of the land and the heavens and technology and the gods, they bound the young man's spirit to his valued possessions.

Old Henry sealed the box with super glue and a lot of faith that nothing could escape. He tied it up in a sling of leather strips and hung it around Narbona's neck.

Three days after the ceremony the guinea pig was still in his body. "So far, so good," Recino said. "No space walks outside the capsule." But Narbona's behavior became erratic. And scary. He wouldn't respond to his name. He shouted he was in the wrong place. He screamed he was living in the wrong skin.

And then he ran away.

Old Henry visited Sandoval. The singer had a face like dry sand and eroded rock. "You must find Narbona. Especially if he's dead. His spirit is bound to the possessions in his pouch. Unless it's released, he can't make the journey to the source of our people."

Sandoval only wanted to solve his own problems. He didn't want to deal with Henry's guilt over a failed experiment. "Recino's the tracker, and he's the one who studies the traditional ways. He knows all about that stuff."

Old Henry shook his head. "That isn't the same as believing."

"How do you know I believe?"

"Do you think your spirit would want to fly if you didn't?" That made no sense to Sandoval.

Old Henry accepted the offer of tea. He pulled out a flask and put a splash into each of their cups. "I'll teach you what must be done."

That was over a thousand miles ago. Sandoval watching Recino toss what few provisions they still had into two nylon packs left over from when such things were easy to come by.

He handed the heaviest stash to Sandoval. "So, what was this mirage you saw?"

Sandoval pointed in the direction they had been tracking Narbona for the past few days. "A tower, the broadcast kind, on a hill. A house and barn and a couple other buildings in a valley."

"I guess this time I'll have to forgive you for being sloppy." Recino trudged off.

Sandoval followed, hoping Narbona sat in the house he had seen, snuggled into an easy chair, drinking a cold beer, waiting to be found. He wished Recino would just keep his mouth shut, but that was as likely as the cold beer.

They reached the top of a bald mound. Sandoval squinted at the bland vista, trying to catch a sliver of sunlight bouncing off the metal tower he'd seen.

In the distance a black tornado erupted into the sky, top foaming like chocolate confection. The world went deeply quiet then exploded with a roar that slammed against the travelers. The mound rippled. Recino and Sandoval staggered. Without moisture to cushion the shockwave, the earth split, tumbling them down the slope in backward somersaults.

Ada Zemke was dozing in her rocking chair on the porch when the blast hit. Road Kill was curled under the low-hanging seat, which drooped more from decades of use than from its occupant's weight. The sudden thunder made her and the chair jump, sending the cat streaking for the barn with a trailing howl of protest. Coming down the elderly woman twisted sideways, banging her butt on the chair's flat arm and flipping the rocker upside down. It landed on top of her, cushion on the wrong end of her anatomy, like a giant cage of a hat.

For a moment she froze unable to believe her undignified position. Through the slats of the porch railing she watched dust from the explosion drift back to earth. Bits of something that had once been alive floated with the black cloud. She hoped one of them lizard things had blown up. She hated them lizard things. They'd first appeared a few months back. The two-foot-long crawlies had no business being in Minnesota, even if the place wasn't what it used to be.

She'd better straighten up and get herself back into that chair before Manny got here. He always showed up after a detonation. Less likely, her granddaughter Deidre might come out of the house and find her with a cushion on her head and rockers in the air.

She pushed the chair upright, still staring at the cloud so she wouldn't miss a second. Stronger than her bony body appeared, she used the railing to haul herself to her feet. Too bad the men in the family hadn't had her strength. Or maybe it was tenacity that had kept her alive this long. Ada's husband and her son-in-law both got the cancer, like so many others. When the weather and everything else went screwy, they just dried up and blew away with the crops.

The women did better. Ada, her daughter, and her granddaughter Deidre weren't touched by the disease, and they out-lasted starvation more than once. It had taken a band of thieving marauders with shotguns to force the life from her daughter. That was before the border bombs were set up for protection. All the horses were stolen during that raid, and everything edible was ripped from the greenhouse. Ada and Deidre mourned, replanted and went on.

The past terrible years had shown Ada something about the mates the women in her blood line chose and the traits those men carried on the Y chromosomes or whatever that male thing was. With luck and Ada's assistance, Deidre would do better. She'd get herself someone with stronger genes, making sure there would be future generations.

Ada's eyes teared from not blinking. The interior of the hazy blossom that still hung in the sky seemed to move on its own. A pattern formed in the airborne soil. It ascended to the peak of the bloom.

A four-legged animal leapt through the sky. Ada rose from her chair along with it. She was sure she saw a snout and eager eyes as the body soared on the updraft. The vision held for a moment then collapsed into random dust. She crumpled too, again finding herself surprised and on the floor.

It took her longer to right herself and longer still to collect her wits. Then Deidre shouted for her, and she had to save her granddaughter from another imaginary crisis. By the time Manny's Jeep topped the western ridge, coming from the direction of the blast as Ada knew it would, she was dignified and ready for company. It was shortly after noon. She rocked in quick jerks, disappointed that she hadn't seen more dusty beasts swirl along the horizon. Still, she possessed a good bit of news, and the audience was delivering himself to her door.

She wouldn't blurt it right out, not a thing like this. She would wait until he asked a leading question, as he always did. She picked at frayed threads on the knee of her jeans and watched Manny ease one of the last operating vehicles in the territory over ruts and around holes, determined to take his sweet time. Maybe she would poke at him a little first, find out if he saw anything unusual when checking the explosion site. Not that she was worried about his believing her. Too many strange things afoot in the world these days for one body to go poo-pooing another.

Manitoba LeClaire parked the Jeep and climbed the porch steps. "Afternoon, Mrs. Zemke." He politely took off his hat and mentally prepared himself to get past the gatekeeper. He wanted to reach Deidre as quickly as possible.

"Good afternoon to you, Manny." She never called him Officer LeClaire, since he had only ended up with the position because Sheriff Olson couldn't find anyone else with the energy to do it. A big strapping fellow once, he was much too thin now. He had taken over patrol duties when the real deputy, Sheriff Olson's nephew Dane, got his head blown off by a defective border bomb. Fortunately, it wasn't one of Deidre's concoctions. Old boozing Jeffers, who frequently suffered DTs since the alcohol supply had become inconsistent, had made it.

The moment Manny removed his hat, Ada got suspicious. He always kept the flat brim low over his eyes while they talked on the porch. He only swept the remnant of a county uniform into his hand when he was ready to go into the house and see Deidre.

"Won't get much out of her today." Ada tried not to show she had noticed the bulge in Manny's jacket pocket. "She's been smoking that nuked-up weed grows out back by the water trough. Goats won't even eat it. That last bunch of tapes you brought been making her crazy-cray."

"We weren't nuked, Mrs. Zemke. You know that." Manny wanted to rush inside, but he felt obligated to exchange at least a few polite words with Grandma Zemke. Here, close to the border, the woman was his best source of information. She felt change in her joints long before Manny caught a hint of it on patrol. And she was lonely.

Her own granddaughter barely spoke to her, or to anyone else except through the radio, which didn't count because it went out to anonymous people instead of communicating face-to-face. Manny knew he'd never get the pair to move into Turtle Creek as long as Deidre felt compelled to run the station and Ada was still healthy enough to keep the farm going.

"Cover up, that's what," Ada said. "The government made up that stuff about carbon dioxide and ozone because they don't want to admit it was one of our bombs that went off and tipped the weather all sideways." And speaking of bombs, she wanted to say; but she wasn't ready to let go of such a great story.

This time Manny let the conspiracy theory pass by without comment. Mrs. Zemke had no patience for explanations and preferred to translate reality into terms she thought she understood. And she thought she understood nuclear war heads. She didn't get how the world's governments were scrubbing the atmosphere, or making it porous so the Earth could breathe again, or however you wanted to describe what they were doing to try to reverse what stupid humans had done to their own environment. He no longer brought it up. Mostly because things had gotten worse. And stranger. He felt it like an itch between his shoulder blades that he couldn't reach.

The official word, when there was any word at all through the slow chain of frequently interrupted communications, continued to be there was no reason to panic. The extreme weather would ease soon. Satellites appropriated to adjust the climate would be returned to their previous functions soon. Computer networks would be available for domestic and commercial use soon.

Would grocery stores be restocked soon? Manny wondered. Would the clinic have medicine soon?

People died waiting for soon.

He'd attended a lot of funerals. He hated not knowing what was going on in the rest of the country and not knowing if anyone realized they needed help out here.

Maybe other places were having enough trouble trying to take care of themselves.

At least land-based radio set ups like Deidre's continued to function. There weren't many of them and their broadcasts were sporadic. The little information Manny received and was able to pass on had to crawl slowly along the beaded string they formed with ham operators. Deidre presented them as Public Service Announcements. "I'd still like to see her."

"She's having a bad day." Maybe she could delay him long enough so he would tell her about the whatever-it-was in his pocket. "She stuck a joint in the microwave. Said it counteracted them radial isotopes or some such thing. Then she went back into her room and smoked it."

"I thought your microwave was broken." Manny fingered the worn brim of the deputy sheriff's hat. He still thought of it as Dane's. Road Kill stuck a crooked head out from under the rocking chair and glowered at him with its one good eye.

"It hasn't been plugged in going on five years." Ada glanced sideways at the pocket. A point threatened to pierce the leather. Could be a corner. Might have something to do with the black cloud. "I don't trust extra stuff hooked into the electrical. Don't know how much wattage it sucks out just sitting there."

Manny nodded silently, avoiding the side trip into the realm of electricity.

"Saw the fireworks." Ada started maneuvering to her own news while hoping it would loosen up Manny about his own. The young man was too heavy-jawed and his nose was too wide for him to be handsome. That hardly mattered anymore. He was male and he was alive—so far. He came from solid stock and showed no signs of the cancer. What more could Deidre possibly want? But her granddaughter's desires were hard to figure.

Deidre's obsession with the radio station made her positively unsociable—like her grandfather in that respect. Ada still enjoyed the mechanics of it but hated the noise. She never listened to it herself. And all that nuked-up weed seemed to leech the sex drive right out of the girl. Getting Manny to keep coming back had become Ada's task.

"Didn't see it." Manny knew he was being held on the porch, a prisoner to good manners. "Heard it though. I was just over at the site. Made a big enough hole." Too big, like there was more punch in it than in a standard bomb. He shook his head. Once he had worn his shiny black hair to his shoulders. Now he kept it buzzed close to the scalp.

"You missed quite a show. Heck of a cloud." Ada clamped her mouth shut, so she wouldn't give it all away without getting a tidbit in return. Manny kept putting a hand to the bulge in his pocket, too distracted to appreciate what she had to tell. She decided to release him. He wasn't going to show her what he had hidden. The only way to get the scoop was through Deidre. "Anyway, she's in her room. You know how to find it without getting lost." Her story was worthy of Manny's undivided attention, so she'd wait until she had it.

But even spectacular news grew stale with time. She would have to catch him on the way out. "Don't expect some big intellectual discussion from her today."

Manny nodded his respects and opened the squeaky screen door. The house wrapped him in cool dusk, and he blinked away the after-images of outside. Mrs. Zemke was methodical in her avoidance of housework. He zigzagged around stacks of technical manuals and piles of cannibalized machines waiting to be moved to the barn.

The box dug into his side. Since finding it at the detonation site, he could think of nothing else. The metal rectangle was probably unimportant, just a subconscious attempt on his part to avoid considering what had tripped the border bomb. Or more precisely, who had tripped it. This time it was no coyote or one of the stunted wolves he'd been seeing lately.

A man had triggered the lethal device.

Drums and chanting came from behind the door to Deidre's bedroom. Manny wrapped softly, knowing she probably couldn't hear him and wouldn't answer if she did. It always made him uncomfortable to let himself into her room, but he could stand in the hall until sunset and she wouldn't notice. He slipped inside, wrinkling his nose at the heavy odor of incinerated weed, and stood with his back against the closed door.

Deidre sat cross-legged on the bed amid pillows and twisted sheets, wrists draped across her knees. Blonde hair fanned her shoulders and fell like a scarf patterned in pale flowers to her waist. Drooping lids fluttered as if in a trance. The drums and chanting abruptly ended. She broke her meditation, eyelids snapping to reveal violet irises surrounded by bloodshot whites. She reached to the bank of electronic equipment stacked beside her bed and flipped a toggle, silencing the room's speakers to prevent feedback. Then she swung a microphone to her mouth.

"That last cut was a song about the *Migizi* Totem, Eagle Totem for those of you who don't speak Ojibwa. If anyone out there knows the exact translation, send it to me by carrier pigeon here at ZEMK, Radio Free Nowhere." Deidre popped out the cassette and slipped in another, her movements elegant and precise. She could swap media in her sleep, and proved it most nights.

Manny had found a collection of neatly labeled cassettes gathering dust at the historical society. The sheriff had sent him to check the garages of abandoned places for stashes of gasoline. He couldn't resist stopping in at the renovated birth place of a forgotten state senator that housed the county's memorabilia. The contents of the cassettes had probably been transferred to various digital media long ago and the originals forgotten. He'd tossed them into his Jeep, knowing Deidre would appreciate them. During the jostling trip to the farm, the flaking glue on the back of the labels had given up and the yellowed papers had peeled off. Deidre matched tapes and titles through random drawings.

She stuck her hand into a cardboard box and pulled out a slip. "And now another number in our continuing Ojibwa marathon. A little ditty about—" Deidre read from the paper, "—'Kewakunah,' 'Homeward Road.'" She fiddled with switches, pushed away the microphone and finally turned to her guest. "This is my favorite."

They were all her favorite. Drums and chanting, same as before to Manny. Having native blood didn't automatically give him an ear for his own culture. Just as having known Deidre for years didn't give him a clue to her thought process.

He'd met her after college when he and Dane moved to Turtle Creek, so Dane could serve as deputy sheriff under his Uncle Louie. Manny got a job at the Olsons' print shop, newspaper and advertising agency. Deidre and her parents and grandparents farmed and operated the radio station. Local merchants liked a few audio spots to go along with their print ads, so Manny set them up. There wasn't much to advertise now.

"The tapes are great," Deidre babbled. "A single song goes on for thirty minutes. Better than 'In-a-gadda-da-vida.' Next time get me some interviews. You know, what it was like in the real olden days before laundry pods and shopping malls. I'll promote them as modern household tips. And don't worry. I do your PSAs every day." She caressed the bright indicator lights. "You know this stuff used to be obsolete. Now it's state of the art."

Deidre laughed, a cackle she knew sounded like marbles bouncing over corrugated metal so she never used it on the air. People were out there listening. She didn't know who, just people. That was enough for her. "I suppose you need another bomb."

"The one that went off today made a bigger hole than usual. It even took out the warning sign. Lucky it didn't trigger a chain reaction. Maybe you did something different?"

She bounced off the bed and stepped over a pile of dirty dishes to reach a tall bureau. The tools she used to repair the eternally malfunctioning equipment littered an old breakfast tray along with stubs of hand-rolled cigarettes with various fillings. While her grandmother made little effort at housekeeping, Deidre made none.

She pulled a bundle of duct tape, wire and tubing from the bottom drawer. "Same as all the rest. You know I wouldn't make a mistake. I only work on them when I'm straight." Not that it took much concentration to put one together. She'd been mixing up explosives since she was a teenager, helping her dad and granddad remove tree stumps. She'd learned to be precise. She could build a device to pop off an ant, or one to turn the whole county into a crater. "Something was really weird about that blast, though. It knocked me off the air for twenty-six minutes. Don't suppose you noticed." Sometimes she sent him messages between cuts, disguised so no one but Manny would know they were for him. He never mentioned them. "It shook loose a connection back in the block house."

Cables curled out her bedroom window in a thick braid held together by duct tape. They ran across the yard to the building that had been the original home of the radio station. It held the rest of the equipment and the connection to the broadcast tower. Much of the space was now taken up by batteries that sucked in excess juice from the solar cells and stored it.

Deidre didn't explain that it had taken her a while to correct the problem because of the little yellow beasties. The chubby creatures had cavorted over the braided wires and scooted under her feet each time she tried to take a step. They'd done it on purpose, too, then giggled and rolled in the dirt while she'd balanced on one foot. Finally, she'd yelled for Gran, who'd scattered them like chickens just by scowling and putting her hands on her hips in that way she had.

Deidre handed Manny the lethal bundle. She noticed the look in his brown eyes. "Not a critter, then."

He nodded, unable to tell her that every time he saw a hole in the dirt he thought of that day he'd gone with Dane to replace a border bomb. He'd leaned against the Jeep to light the last cigarette from the pack. He'd turned away from the wind so the stick wouldn't burn too fast, putting his back to Dane. The two of them would share it on the drive back to town as soon as his friend, his best friend, his only friend, took care of this one little duty.

Deidre shrugged. "Well, that's what they're supposed to do. Keep us safe from scavengers who'll otherwise murder us in our sleep."

What a waste, Manny wanted to say, to blow up people just because they're strangers. But words rarely made it out of his mouth when he was with Deidre. Instead he freed the box from his pocket and held it out to her.

"A souvenir?" Deidre asked. Manny winced and she was sorry she had spoken, as she often was when face-to-face with a real person. Barely an inch thick and twice as long as wide, the black rectangle covered her small hand. She flopped it from palm to palm. Then she put it to her ear and gave it a shake.

Manny grabbed her arm to stop her, surprising them both. His hand wrapped around her thin wrist, and he wondered if she ever really ate a complete meal, not the odds and ends he saw scraps of on the dirty plates. "Sorry." But he didn't let go. "It's just that I've felt—strange—since I picked it up. Protective, sort of."

"You choose unusual things to care about."

He released her and unsuccessfully fought a blush. I'm not the only one, he wanted to say.

Diedre grabbed one of her tools. "It rattled. At least two things inside. I can puncture it then use metal clippers. It should be easy to get open."

Manny nodded. "I think that's why I brought it here." The chanting from the radio equipment started to fall into a pattern for him. The cadence seemed familiar, almost like a pulse.

Radio waves carried the rhythm from the farm out across the barren countryside. Within its circle Recino and Sandoval clambered to the top of another mound. The rolling landscape had seemed endless, but now they looked down into the valley Sandoval had discovered while dead.

Recino scrunched up his face. "You hear anything?"

"Maybe." For the past three miles the sound of drums had pounded at him like they were inside his head. He'd said nothing, afraid of getting teased if he heard them and Recino didn't. The tumble from the blast had scraped the left side of his face bloody. Gravel was embedded in both palms. His back felt like a single giant bruise.

"Not Navajo." Recino bore his own badges from the fall. An egg swelled from his forehead, and he favored his right hip.

"How can you tell?"

"My spirit knows."

It was Recino's standard flippant answer. Yeah, as if you had a spirit, Sandoval thought. Why couldn't the guy just admit he knew all that stuff because he'd studied native cultures for years. Fatigue stiffened his legs, but he refused to stop, afraid he would nod off and leave his body again. As the drums intensified, so did the sensation that he was about to slip.

They started down into the valley. A Jeep sat close to the house. Other buildings clustered nearby. Barn, shed, greenhouses, a square structure with a flat roof. Tilted banks of solar cells flanked the scene. A fenced section abutting the barn contained slow-moving cows. No horses. Sandoval wished there were horses. The pickup had given out in what he thought was South Dakota. Hard to say exactly where. They'd traded the truck carcass for skinny nags that hadn't lasted long before they collapsed from thirst, malnutrition, over-work, depression—take your pick. Still, he really wished there were horses.

He stumbled toward the farm, fearing it might never get any closer no matter how long he moved toward it. Like a mirage. Like one of those dreams where you keep doing something over and over but make no progress. Like how life had become. Happily, the structures gained size until a porch stretched before him like a great grinning mouth full of discolored teeth with a gap where stairs stuck out.

A rocking chair bobbed as if recently abandoned. "Hello." Chanting pelted Sandoval like rain. He stood in the dirt, not daring to put a foot on the bottom step. He'd heard stories. In some places they shot you through shuttered windows without a civilized how-do-you-do.

A banshee wail scraped across his nerves. At the top of the stairs a demon cat spit and clawed the air. In the misshapen skull one green eye stared down at him while a milky gray marble beside it was not quite watching Recino.

"Didn't know anything could be that ugly," Recino called to the house. "If you're mutants, you can stay where you are and we can shout back and forth." He paused, waiting for a reply. The cat settled into a low growl. "We're looking for someone. Lost signs of him near here. He's a little crazy. Not dangerous or anything. We need to take him back home."

Manny observed the two men through a curtained window. No sign of weapons. Their skin coloring, like his own, went deeper than tan. They wore the lean appearance of travelers managing on rations. One had on a bright orange vest with tubing sprouting from it, like a spacey deer hunter or an under-water road construction worker. They must have crossed the border at the explosion site. It was the only gap in the defensive barrier. When they mentioned the crazy man, Manny felt his gut twist. The cause of the blast was no longer an anonymous stranger. Now it was a person with friends who cared enough to chase him across a land that had become indifferent to its inhabitants. They deserved to know what had happened.

Ada stood at another window, pistol ready, a .454 Casull she was especially fond of because it didn't have a safety. Deidre stayed in her room, uninterested in the visitors until she was sure they were real.

Manny put on his hat and tugged the brim to his brow. He stepped onto the porch, reluctant to perform this part of his official duty. He hoped the men would understand about the border, even if Manny doubted the wisdom of it himself. If they attacked him in a rage for the death of their friend, Ada would protect him. From the marks on their faces, he wondered if they'd already been in a fight.

Manny introduced himself and got their names in return. "You look like you argued with something that argued back."

The one named Recino pointed a thumb over his shoulder, "Got shook around by an explosion."

Manny frowned and motioned them up the stairs. "I've got bad news." He nudged Road Kill with his boot. The cat slithered under the rocker, continuing to sound like a crop duster in need of engine repair. They settled into wooden chairs on the other side of the porch, away from the cat.

Manny explained, trying to be direct enough so the men understood but euphemistic enough to show respect. When he finished, Recino scratched his head, careful to avoid the discolored lump. "So that firecracker was Lloyd Narbona becoming one with the ozone. At least there's no corpse."

Sandoval hung his head and sobbed.

Manny massaged his knuckles, uncomfortable with the ravine between the two reactions. "I'm sorry," he said to Sandoval. "You must have been close."

Recino shrugged. "It's not that. He's thinking about his wife. Some people been having sort of a medical problem lately. Doc Rita, she runs the clinic, and Old Henry, our singer, tried this treatment on Narbona. It seemed to work, but then he started acting nuts and ran off. We were supposed to bring him back, so they could figure out what went wrong." Recino dug a finger into his ear. "You got your old Anishinaabe grandfather in that house mumbling away?"

Unconsciously, Manny pressed back in his chair. "Medical?" The community had enough problems without a disease.

Recino noticed the reaction. "Not contagious. I've been traveling with Sandoval, here, practically across the whole continent and I didn't catch it. Doc Rita says it's one of those things like the cancer that either happens to a person or doesn't." He gave Sandoval a disgusted look. "Although it appears the condition can get worse."

"Maybe we can help." It was an empty offer. The hospital had little, but Manny felt a responsibility. He was the one who'd set the border bomb that had obliterated the person who might have provided a cure for this unspecified, mysterious ailment.

"Not likely," Recino said.

A spasm rippled through Sandoval. He sagged chest to knees and rolled limp to the floor. Manny jumped forward and checked for a pulse.

Recino pushed him aside. "Just sit back and watch the show." He unclipped a plunger from the back of the vest. He checked that its tubing was securely connected to the front. Then he worked the pump, just the way Doc Rita had taught him. Down up. Down up. Soon he was following the beat of the music in his head. "Look around while you're up there. Any sign of Narbona?"

Sandoval's eyelashes fluttered. "He's a wolf now. He's bound. He can't leave."

Recino sat back on his heels. "The spirit pouch survived the blast?" He looked to Manny.

"The only thing I found was a box." Manny described the container. Recino nodded confirmation. They hoisted Sandoval back into his chair.

Tormented by curiosity, Ada decided to take charge. She marched onto the porch and curtly introduced herself. "Now, Mr. Recino, you better provide some details, because I saw something in that explosion that needs explaining."

Without argument Recino accepting her as holder of the real authority here—either her or the Casull leveled at him. "Darndest thing, lately some people been having trouble staying in their bodies. Some don't mind so much and have better control than others. Sandoval, here, thinks his wife Althea is swapping places with her little sister, who's unmarried and popular with the young studs. Althea has her fling then switches back, and who's to say if it's adultery or not." He left out the part that gave him the creeps so bad he couldn't even tease Sandoval about it.

If you really looked at it—trying not to think of them as people you'd known your whole life—it was like a horror flick. A loose spirit leaves its lifeless body and goes into someone else's flesh. Which has just been vacated by its owner, who is moving into your corpse. It was the dead possessing the dead. Like demons. Like zombies without decaying skin falling off. It didn't matter that they went back into their own bodies afterward. Had Althea or any of them really done it? With everyone acting so crazy, how would you be able to tell?

Ada was uninterested in domestic gossip. "Mr. Recino, who are this Docrita and Mr. Henry Singer?" She refused to refer to age or to include the middle initial of R, as this man always did for some unfathomable reason.

"Singer's not Old Henry's name. It's what he is. *Hataali.* Our singer. A medicine man." Recino gave his head a shake. "Now I'm hearing Navajo. There must be some inter-tribal council going on in your house." He translated the words pulsing in his head. "'We are Dineh. We are The People.'"

"The Wolf's pissed." Sandoval trembled from his latest death and from Recino sharing his private shame with strangers. At least Big Mouth didn't know all of what he suspected. There were stories that sex partners were changing places with one another. He was almost certain Althea had inhabited a man and let him into her body, her own or whichever one she was using, so they could—.

A man who wasn't him.

She'd never invited her own husband, who should be closer to her than anyone, to switch places with her and make love together. That's what sent pain through him like a knife between his ribs.

He shivered and tried to shove it far from his thoughts, but it wouldn't leave. Narbona was a special friend of Althea's younger sister. He might have been one of those men. "The Wolf's really pissed. He doesn't have a body, but his life here won't let him go. He can't make the journey down the mountain trail to the underworld where the Dineh dwelled before they came to the surface of the Earth." Did he know that or was the signing in his head telling him? Was that Narbona's voice?

Manny pushed back his hat and massaged a temple. "Damn, I'm feeling it too."

"Nonsense. You can't hear the radio out here." Ada was upset at herself for missing the chance to tell Manny about the leaping animal in the black cloud. Now it was too late, only a footnote to the sudden appearance of strangers, the box that must have been the object in Manny's pocket, and native chanting from nowhere trying to take over her mind. Events should spread themselves out, not bunch up so each one loses its impact in the mess.

"Gran!" Deidre's wail shredded the air.

Firm grip on her pistol, Ada sprinted into the house. The others followed into Deidre's bedroom, Recino and Manny supporting Sandoval.

An angry dirge assaulted the room, base voice punching out syllables. Deidre knelt on the bed, pounding the tape deck with a fist, her bloodshot eyes wide. "The cassette won't eject. Gran, get him out of my signal."

"Turn it off, dear."

"I did! Every switch."

Lights still glowed from the panels. Recino put his share of Sandoval's weight onto Manny and stepped over debris to the bank of electronics. He plucked the metal box from the top of the dusty deck. An irregular opening snipped through the lid exposed the interior. Inside was an iridescent blue butterfly preserved in a thin square of clear plastic. Beside it rested a tuft of fur wrapped in a leather cord. Recino was pretty sure it had been clipped from the pelt Narbona kept wrapped around his rifle. He stuck a finger into the spirit pouch to poke at it. The interior was cold as a human cadaver. He snapped his hand back. "What else was in here?"

Deidre pointed to her equipment. "A cassette. It's got a commercial label, *Abbey Road*." She gestured to the voice-filled room. "When I played it, this came out."

"Well, I'll be a plaid chameleon." Recino couldn't remember the name of the group. The apprentice singer loved their music and fancied himself a collector. He had their work in every form from digital to old vinyl. He subjected everyone within miles of his blaring truck speakers to their songs. This definitely wasn't them. It was Narbona, chanting away with a vengeance. Guess Old Henry knew his stuff, although it seemed his solution to the loose-spirit problem needed a lot more work. "Lady, you've got yourself a haunted radio station."

Sandoval straightened, removing himself from Manny's support. He put a hand to his chest. "I feel—solid." The medallion pressed into his palm through his thin cotton tee shirt. "The Wolf's reciting the chant Old Henry used to connect him to his pouch. He's binding our spirits."

Road Kill darted into the room and vaulted into Ada's arms. She cradled the cat and the gun in crooked elbows. "Binding them to what?"

"Whatever you care about, identify with." Panic edged Sandoval's words. "Whatever you think of as being part of you. You'll be bound to it forever, even after you die. We'll all be ghosts anchored to the earth like Narbona, for eternity."

Recino gently set the box on the bed. "Guess there are worse things than dying. Narbona wants to make sure others suffer with him."

Deidre had lost track of the conversation. All she heard

was the chanting. It didn't seem so terrible now. The intensity pulled her in and was comforting in an exotic way. She pressed her cheek against the microphone, eyes closed, blissful smile on her pale lips.

Manny rubbed his forehead under the brim of his hat. He didn't exactly believe, but he had seen plenty while growing up so he couldn't disbelieve. Spirit pouch or not, he'd experienced an odd sensation the moment he'd touched the cool metal. Now he realized he should have questioned finding it at all, considering the miles covered by the residue of the explosion.

The chanting demanded Manny's attention with the compelling rhythm of his own heartbeat. He tried to fight it. He had to think this through. Everyone in the room was being affected. Everyone who heard the bitter voice.

Fear struck him. It wasn't just in this house. The singing flew out on the airwaves. Others were hearing it, too. His neighbors. Dane's family. If conditions were right, maybe as far away as what used to be the Twin Cities. If the strangers were telling the truth, if they were right, all those people, who relied on the radio to keep them informed, to keep them connected to humanity, were being chained to things around them. They were destined after death to haunt the world, as malicious as this Wolf.

Dane's hat pressed against his brow. He shared a responsibility for this. But it really didn't matter who caused what. His job was to protect, no matter what crazy, incomprehensible circumstances came along. He had to stop the broadcast.

Manny tore Deidre from the equipment and threw her, screaming, onto the bed so he could get past her to the cables that snaked out the window. He ripped at layer after layer of silver tape and black tape and silver tape that held the bundle of patched wiring together. Over the decades Ada and then Deidre had built linkages too strong to dismantle in an instant. An inward spiral, like a churning tornado, sucked at his strength. Duty kept him going.

Deidre had said something about the explosion knocking the station off the air, about it shaking something loose in the block house. Manny climbed out the window. Once flowering shrubs had lined this wall. Now he landed on barren ground and a few of the new, tougher dandelions that you couldn't kill but you could eat. Each one was a perpetual salad. He followed the cables to what had once been a green, overgrown yard.

He scooped up the thick, dusty braid and tugged, taking out the slack. Then he raised the serpent and slammed it sharply against the ground, cracking it like a whip. He felt the vibration travel along the column. The connection held. Again he snapped the line, fighting an urge to relax into the sucking spiral of the chant that still pounded through his body.

A blackness appeared in the air above him, blocking out sunlight. He looked up into the cold eyes of a canine, teeth bared, claws curled to strike. The creature was ethereal, composed not of flesh and fur but of dust raised from the battered, naked land.

The wolf howled, creating an angry whirl. It exploded in Manny's brain. A gust caught the brim of the deputy sheriff's hat, Dane's hat, and tore it from his head. He dropped the cable and covered his ears, but the shriek continued to scrape at him, drowning out the roar of the wind.

The sooty cloud loomed over him. A claw stretched down and raked across his cheek. The pain reached deep into his soul. He felt the wolf try to leap into him, to possess him. It would be easy to let it. There had been enough times since Dane's death when he'd wanted to just let go.

Something always stopped him. He told himself it was the job, Dane's job, that forced him to get up every morning and patrol Turtle Creek and what was left of the county. Maybe at first it was. But there was a deeper reason that he didn't have a name for, that was completely selfish. He wanted to live for something because he didn't want to die.

With the wolf slashed at him, Manny lunged for the silver-stripped snake. It was gritty in his sweating hands. Again he tugged. Again he slammed the braid into the hard ground, feeling no release. He threw every ounce of his muscle and bulk against it. He dug his heels into the hard earth.

Ada was suddenly behind him. And the two strangers. And Deidre. They struggled together, through the wind and spiraling grit, in a tug-of-war against the malicious spirit. They strained with their weight and the persistence that had kept them alive during the past hard years. They fought with their hunger and frustration and disappointment at another planting that failed to thrive, at another dear one who'd left them more alone.

Something gave way. The sudden release tumbled them backward to the ground.

The wind calmed. The tornado hung motionless. The individual particles separated from the mob. They drifted away or settled back into the soil. Above them the Wolf receded with a fading wail, leaving a stark silence. Manny put a hand to his face, sure it would come away bloody. He felt the sting in his mind, but there was no gash, not even a welt, where the claws had wounded him.

Sandoval absently rubbed at his medallion. "He lost his

voice, but he's still here. He can't leave unless we help him."

They built a small pyre on the black desert. The cassette slid out of the tape deck easily now. They placed the box and its items on the wooden platform. A dust devil buzzed around them, annoying but not menacing. Recino batted at it. "So, Narbona had to take on the wolf. He couldn't have picked the butterfly." He set the wood aflame.

Sandoval spoke the words Old Henry had taught him.

When the leaping fire settled into coals and it seemed safe, Ada, Diedre and Manny got the station back on the air.

Night came and the moon rose orange over the eastern hills.

From the porch Ada and Manny watched the last of the embers. Diedre slotted "In-a-gadda-da-vida" and joined them in the fresh evening air.

Ada rocked, Road Kill curled in her lap. The Casull rested on the floorboards at her side. "Bunch of nonsense." What would her spirit bind to anyway? Making it through another day was what mattered. Others had died because they'd mourned the loss of this thing or that thing. She was alive because she didn't let it bother her to do without, like Road Kill here, who managed with one eye and just enough of a brain to not give up.

Deidre half-sat on the railing, one foot swinging and the other on the floor for stability. She gazed at the two figures silhouetted against the glow that seemed reluctant to fade. She didn't care about binding spirits. Hers had been bound for a long time to the station, and the sounds she broadcast, and the people she reached out to. "Think we stopped it? Whatever it was—in time? For us and for everyone?" Maybe she could convince Manny to move out here with her.

"Personally, I'm not taking any chances." Manny descended the stairs to the barren earth. The invisible wound on his cheek still stung. He squatted and took off his hat, Dane's hat. He thought it was lost forever, but Road Kill had dragged it back from somewhere and presented it to him like a trophy, the same way he would a dead rabbit. Strange cat. He stripped off the sheriff insignia and the leather band. The soft felt tore easily along the sweat marks.

He placed the pieces in a pile. From his shirt pocket he took a book of matches. He hadn't had a cigarette in a long time, but he still carried the folder with the name of a bar in Fargo where he and Dane used to hang out. Perhaps he should make a short speech, something about release and freedom. Nothing came to him. Well, he wasn't much for words.

He struck a flame and held it to a ragged edge. The scraps ignited in a whoosh. He leaned back from the unexpected inferno and plopped into the dirt.

"This stuff always knocks me on my butt too." Recino was standing over Manny. Vanes of yellow light danced across him. "Darndest thing, sticks itself right in my face and I still can't believe, not really." He tapped his chest with a fist. "Not in here." He offered a hand and helped Manny to his feet. "We'll be leaving at sunrise. That's Sandoval's idea, not mine. He's eager to get back to that wandering wife of his. Appreciate it if you'd guide us out so we don't end up like Narbona."

Manny brushed dirt from his jeans and nodded. "I can take you up to the border in the Jeep and show you where it's safe to walk through. I'm sure Mrs. Zemke has a vegetable or two she can spare from the greenhouse to send along with you."

Sparks shot upward from the burning hat, forming lace in the hot air. Tomorrow Manny would deliver the men to safety. Then he would go to town, to Dane's Uncle Louie, and resign. There were plenty of other things that needed doing. Maybe the border was necessary. Maybe it wasn't. He would no longer be the one to keep it functioning. His spirit wouldn't let him.

Recino said good night and wandered toward the barn to find a place to bed down. Manny returned to the porch and put his arm around Deidre. She smiled at him in shock. Ada gave him an it's-about-time look.

Sandoval stood alone before what was left of the fire. The medallion felt like a slice of moonlight against his chest. Just to be sure, he again softly chanting the words Old Henry had taught him to help Narbona on his journey. He'd record it for Deidre so she could broadcast it, in case there were some listening spirits who needed release. He didn't know if that would be as potent as saying it in person. This spirit stuff, like the rest of life, seemed to be a lot of guess work and a lot of hope. He wasn't must of a guesser. But he was getting better at the hope part.

The Night Lives Immense

The night lives immense, darkly drifting.
Drifting quiet. Absorbed and scattered
through the cells of quiet, infused through

the universe. I float over stars
without burning, playing with planets,
colored marbles that roll soft in my
palm. I have hot, dim burnings of old

fires, the blues and yellows wrapped in
thin swirling spheres. They roll soft in my
palm. I should throw them thick into the
sun, engulfed. I should swallow them whole.

But I bring them close in my closed fist,
precious stones of time and a life that
won't let go, that clings and scars like skin.

Roar at the Heart of the World

I remember the day the world changed. Not by a date or a time or by any number. I remember it by the low voices of men in dusty boots who hunched over the table on our veranda and drank gin and tonic. I remember it by the dry wind through the weaving grass and the red-maned lion's roar. I remember because that day Africa changed. And Africa was my world.

"One man dead and a war begins." Young Mr. Finch tapped the side of his glass but ignored its contents. "South Africa seems so far away, and yet—. If only they hadn't killed him."

"They were looking for an excuse," Mr. Kreshenko said, his Romanian inflection rumbled deep from a round chest. "Any would do, but they got about the best possible. The real reasons are more complex—economics, dignity, power, ego. So it has always been. This is only the lit match tossed onto the pile of straw."

Poor Mr. Finch. Thin and pale, he seemed unsuited to the wilderness of the Kenyan highlands, newly reopened to foreign ownership a century after the remnants of the first settlers were expelled. "The blaze is out of control," he muttered. "What will we do when it reaches us?"

From my child-sized chair at my child-sized table set a short distance from the adults' furnishings I searched the horizon for the glow of flames. I sniffed the air for smoke. I listened to the animals for panic. A fire is a frightening thing in a land that gives water more by whim than season. Beyond the veranda the night was black and still. I heard my dog Orion patrolling the stable. In their boxes the horses dreamed of familiar things. In the hills a leopard circled its prey without a sound. They did not know of a fire. Not then.

I bent over my paper and finished covering the flaming yellow with black. Africa was like the drawing I made. A layer of coloured patches—red, blue, green, every pigment in the crayon box—then a dark layer covering it like the night. The wax sticks grew soft in the hot day. I kept them in a cool place and took them out after sunset. In the brittle light from the battery-powered torch I scratched off a design of hills and wattle trees, antelope and grasses. The colours beneath the black appeared in sudden vividness.

"Hah!" Mr. Haugen gave a single sharp laugh. "We'll be murdered in our beds by the natives, that's what."

I fussed with my crayons while I pulled the meaning from his thick German accent. The Romanian spoke like the ocean; I floated on the rolling rhythm. But the German ground out his words, and I had to pick through the rubble.

"Hush, you'll frighten the child." Finch touched me with a concerned look, quick as a feather.

"Frighten Lizzy?" my father said. He leaned against a post that supported the slanting roof of the veranda and swirled the liquid in his glass. "Lizzy stalks wild boar with the Nandi hunters. A little war won't frighten her."

No. I was not afraid. I was not afraid of the far away fire. I was not afraid of a war, barely knew what one was. There was history of course, but Father had little interest in the past and I had less, having less past to be interested in. He told me nothing of wars, except that there had been some. I was too young to read the thick books wrapped in tooled leather. When I did read, it was about horses.

Togom told me about the many battles between the Nandi and the Masai. But that was different. Both warrior tribes, it was their heritage to fight. Tribe against tribe. Not Black against White as in the war my father and his friends whispered about.

I preferred the stories of great hunts. A hunter armed with spear and shield against a lion was braver than human against human—be it with spears or guns. There was little challenge in an opponent who had the same kind of strength, the same weapons, the same thoughts as you, whether or not the skin was the same colour.

But a lion thinks differently from a human, and a leopard thinks differently from a lion. Each animal is a separate challenge: That is the essence of the hunt.

"They can't force us out," my father said. "It's only an excuse to take back the land now that we've paid for it and spent four years proving we're not crazy, that it can produce."

"It isn't just the Kenyan government," Finch said. "England and all the other countries have told their citizens to leave. Burton," he said to my father, "you received your notice officially signed by his royal majesty the same time I did."

"And what would I do back in Germany?" Haugen asked the insects buzzing around the spots of light hanging from the bare rafters. "Can't raise coffee there. My older brother inherited the family vineyard. That's why I came here in the first place. Invested my meager inheritance in the land. Now they want me to leave. Burton, not to minimize your situation, but at least you can train horses anywhere, even back in England. You still have connections there."

My father's chin was set with a determination I knew well. "And what about the mill? I have contracts to deliver flour."

"There may not be anyone to deliver the flour to," the German said.

"Well," Finch said with forced vigor, "Diana and I haven't been here that long. We still have investments in London and a little money. Of course this isn't the way I planned—." He let it trail off. Nothing seemed to turn out as he planned. "You're staying then, Burton?"

I pretended absorption in my artwork. As if there was any doubt, I thought.

"Yes."

"Suspected you'd feel that way." Finch stared at the table cut from the cedar forest a short distance behind the house. "Burton, Diana and I talked it over. This war is going to be tough, no other way about it. And—I hope you won't think me critical—Elizabeth is beyond the age when most girls begin formal schooling. And you know that we adore her. We practically think of her as our own, especially since the baby—. Diana and I would like to take her back to England with us, just until things are settled here or until you decide to come home. It makes perfect sense, really.

"Damn it," he said with more weariness than strength. "I'm trying to make it sound so noble, as if we'd be doing you a favor. Truth is, it would break Diana's heart to be separated from Lizzy. Mine too, I'm afraid."

My father showed no surprise. Since my mother died

when I was two years old, people who wanted to take me away from him had lined up like mismatched beads on a string. Each argued that it was for my own good. I should have been too young, yet I remember every one.

A particularly ugly bead—one of my mother's aunts I think, in a wide hat covered with impossibly large net flowers—proclaimed that with her social contacts and careful guidance I would "get on in the world very nicely" and probably "marry above my station." But her real thoughts were simple and close to the surface. She wanted a little princess buried in taffeta flounces to show off to her friends. As always, Father politely declined the offer.

No previous bead was as honest as Finch, few were as nice. Still, I was surprised when my father said, "I'll think about it."

What was there to think about? Of England I remembered only starched dresses, tight shoes, overly-perfumed relatives in stuffy rooms, and boredom.

I belonged to Africa. Finch and his equally porcelain wife could no more uproot me, transplant me in British soil and expect me to thrive than they could a bamboo tree. And yet I heard my father say, "I'll think about it."

The guests left. Kreshenko and Finch lived the farthest away on farms with a common border, their houses still kilometers apart. Haugen was our closest neighbor, but he lived on the other side of the wide Rongai Valley, quite a distance by road, a bit less cross-country. The headlights of their tough, battered vehicles caught the eyes of animals along the edge of the ruts that served as a road.

Do not move, I told them. The noisy motor-beasts will soon rumble past and be gone.

"If war was an animal, I would hunt it and kill it," I told Sayid that night when he tucked me into bed. The Somali served as housekeeper and nanny. He was one of the colours of Africa that I tried to capture in my drawings. Unknown to outsiders. Unseen unless you scratched the continent's surface. His face was grim in the pale glow from the lamp on the narrow table beside my bed. "It would not let you, Lizzy. It is not a natural beast."

I leaned over the edge of my little cot and gave Orion's brown and white coat a pat goodnight. A fusion of hard muscle and simple mind, he stood waist high to my child body. My father made him for me, so he was of no discernible breed. He sauntered to the end of the bed, respectfully avoiding Sayid who was a Muslim and could not touch or be touched by a dog, and curled up on his rug. I didn't think of him as big, for as the years passed he seemed to shrink. But I suppose that my own growth caused it to seem so and that he was larger than most dogs.

Sayid pressed the button that turned off the light. He stepped out of the room, leaving a trail of spice and soft rustles. As every night since we have lived in this little house, he left the door tilted open the width of his hard, narrow body, so I would not be alone, so he could slip in if I cried out in my sleep. To my knowledge, I never did.

For a moment I listened to the animals—Orion at the foot of the bed, the horses in their boxes, the large cats prowling, the slim eland sleeping yet watchful for the cats. I never heard the smaller animals—the chickens in our coop, my pair of chameleons in their cage. Either the smaller animals spoke in voices too soft for my sense or their tiny brains made no noise.

Only rarely did I hear humans. Perhaps their thoughts were too deep within them and too complex. I especially never heard my father. Perhaps he could protect himself from my intrusion.   Usually I had other ways of knowing his thoughts.

Because of the company, I had been allowed to stay up past my bedtime. Drowsiness crept in and enveloped me sooner than I expected, so I had no time to consider the adults' concerns about this far away war. As was my habit every night, I consciously stopped listening. Otherwise the animals kept me awake with their triumphs of life and screams of death. I was instantly asleep.

In the morning before a proper dawn had the chance to announce the day I took my knife and spear and slipped out of the house with Orion at my side. The cool air bit my legs below the khaki shorts, nipped my arms exposed by the brief sleeves of my blouse. Soon my father would be up to begin the daily work with the race horses. I wanted to be gone so he could not turn me back to my neglected lessons in grammar and arithmetic. Like the horses, I, too, had daily work.

In all other things my father allowed me the freedom of a sprite, an independence that shocked the other farmers and gave Sayid nervous fits. But my studies were carefully monitored, and I received scoldings for hunting when my lessons had shown no progress. I was a child and endured them with a penitent bow but without remorse or the resolve never to do it again.

The banks of solar panels sat expectantly beside the mill, tilted toward the point of sunrise, ready to power the machinery. Shiny solar flats, similar to the others but portable, leaned against the building. Each morning Kitau, one of the Kikuyu workers, set them up as needed to recharge the batteries for the lamp in my room, and the torches that we relied on at night for the veranda and the stable.

Wheat stalks swayed in the field, each slim plant reaching

above my head. Beside the golden spears, Father's prized patch of genetically enhanced maize rustled with health. Less tall than the wheat, its thick shafts supported a heavy crop that my father was already using as a wonderful excuse to plan a party for harvest. Farther up in the hills there was a cluster of coffee trees, the traditional crop of the area left over from the first wave of European settlers long ago. My father's nature rebelled at tradition, but I think their untended survival intrigued him. He fussed over the plot as if it were nature's equivalent of his maize.

I traveled over the hill and into the valley. Three hundred meters below, smoke from the Nandi village drifted up in thin lines that converged into one then faded. I descended through the half light at the edge of day. The mongrel dogs yapped at my approach. They were ill-mannered and barked at everything. Orion refused to answer their coarseness with anything but silence. They shared an inherited memory; but because of his mixed genes, Orion felt no kinship with them.

Togom and Ruta ducked out of their huts and greeted me. They each wore a *shuka*. The single piece of cloth wrapped under one arm, sloped across the chest and back and was knotted at the opposite shoulder.

Togom gave Orion a pat. The motion seemed a wasteful use of the strength stored in his lean muscles, but the fluid body, like shadowed water, craved movement. "How are the animals this morning?" he asked me in Swahili.

I wasn't fluent in Nandi, but Swahili was accepted as a common language. The Kavirondo and Kikuyu workers on the farm used it. I spoke it better than I did English, which appalled the fragile Mrs. Finch. I could substitute a few Nandi, Kikuyu, even Masai words if they fit my purpose. "Nervous," I said. Did I describe them or myself? Although it dominated my thoughts, I didn't say that my father might send me away.

Togom, the village's *ol-oiboni*, spiritual leader, nodded. "The sun quivers, afraid to come out." His soul grew from this land. He didn't need me to tell him how the animals felt, so I knew it was a lesson. He recognized my distraction. He wished me to stay alert, to push deeper into my sensitivity.

Ruta shook his head. His shoulders were wide for a Nandi, and he carried more weight on his round chest than Togom. But he was just as quick with a spear. *"Mbaisa sana,"* terribly bad, he said. "This is not good for hunting."

"Ahh, but we have Elisbet to tell them not to be so, to say they die honourable deaths on *murani* spears," Togom said.

I knew the other message in his words. I am *ol-oiboni*, he said, I can do much but this I cannot do: I cannot make the animals hear me. Only you can do this, Elisbet.

Togom motioned. A girl no older than my eight years dressed in a skirt of skins that brushed her ankles brought three gourds of blood and curdled milk.

In the village there is no division between life and ceremony, living and religion. Solemnly we observed the pre-hunt ritual. We each took a gourd and drank in turn, chanting praise to the blood of the bull. Togom first as leader. Then Ruta. Then me, Orion respectfully sitting at my feet.

The girl watched me because it was not allowed for her eyes to touch the men. Nandi women do not hunt. I'm sure she wondered how I dared to stand beside the strong warriors and drink warm bull's blood, how I dared to lift a spear against a boar. I had no answers for her unasked questions. Only that it seemed natural to hunt and that I wasn't afraid with Togom and Ruta and Orion.

Togom and Ruta hefted their spears and shields. Morning

blossomed across the flat sky. In this part of Africa, so near the equator, the sky is very close to the earth. I imagined that when I grew as tall as a *muran*, I would be able to stand on Mount Kenya and stretch my fingertips to touch the blue.

We crossed a pasture crowded with indulged cattle. The uncircumcised boys who tended them watched covertly as we passed. When we cleared the worst of the slippery dung, we ran in single file. The floor of the long, winding valley is always clogged with foliage and impassible from one end to the other. Togom led us up over the lip then along the perimeter of the Mau Forest. We descended back into the Rongai as the sun rose. I listened.

Impala, eland, kongoni—all to the sides of us, all scattered. And below us—

"Boar," I said, trying not to let my excitement rattle my voice, trying to be a calm hunter. "But it is too quiet between here and there."

We reached the jumble of rocks where water trickled through the scarlet dust, turning it to sucking clay. In the heat, mist rose from the puddle that formed.

Mist. The Masai word is *E-rukenya*. Kenya.

The meager watering-hole was always populated with sleek impala, eland, zebras. I saw nothing except the indentations of hooves and paws in the clay. I heard nothing.

Togom and Ruta froze, experience guiding them. In imitation, I stood still. Orion moved in front of me. He sniffed the ground, the air. His thoughts danced bright and expectant.

"*Simba*," I whispered. "Orion tells me this."

"Ahh," Ruta whispered back, "the one with the red mane who will not talk to you."

"It must be," I said.

"But you can talk to it," Togom said. "Say that today we do not hunt lion. Say that we hunt boar."

In my mind I repeated Togom's message to the invisible animal. I sent the thought across the crimsons and coppers of the clearing, into the tawny grass and skeletal brush that clawed the stones, not knowing if I was heard.

From the deep, cool shadow of an overhanging rock, drifted a huge golden cat, a muted color of Africa silently revealed. It shook the cinnamon halo surrounding its head and flicked its cinnamon-tipped tail with impatience. The steady eyes evaluated Togom. Then Ruta. Then Orion. I cried to the dog to hold. The lion's stare was a challenge. Orion's every muscle tightened to spring. He was furious with me for the restraint.

The lion's eyes slid to me. The stare burned and chilled. "I know you," the eyes said, although I heard nothing.

The lion's eyes returned to Togom—leader of *murani, oloiboni.* This beast had no time for lesser beings, such as Ruta, Orion and myself.

Togom raised his shield and held his spear ready, but he already battled the lion with a returned stare. "He is angry with us for disturbing him," he said calmly, almost mockingly to shame the lion. I knew the cat did not speak to him. Togom read the animal's stance and breathing and eyes. Face to face with an adversary, he did not need my assistance. He understood the lion's thoughts because they were both warriors, both proud.

A lion saunters with a lazy economy, but it charges with speed and conviction. If the red-maned beast attacked, it would seriously rip apart or kill at least one of us. But it could not win. Together the two *murani* would bring it down. And in my youth I imagined that I could play a role in this, too.

Certainly Orion, who saw all encounters with cats as great sport, would do his share. Still, the cold of one of us dead or nearly dead—

I repeated the message because it was all I could do. I was certain it heard, but I feared it did not listen.

The lion claimed a step of ground toward us. I held my spear ready. Now I saw wet patches on the lion's paws. Blood. It had a fresh kill nearby, one worth protecting if only to protect its honour.

I squinted against the sunlight to peer into the shadow behind the lion. A slain boar, the hide shredded by a dozen slashes, stained the crimson soil darker.

We will kill our own boar, I told the lion with false bravado. We are hunters, not hyenas who take from others.

I saw no change in the lion, but Togom quietly said, "Let us leave this place."

We moved away from the water-hole. Ruta and I did not ask Togom how he knew that the lion had decided not to attack. The beast watched our cautious retreat then went back to its kill.

Orion was especially valiant in our quest for a boar, putting all of his frustration over the lost cat into it. Ruta brought down a large one with his spear and Orion ripped out its throat, suffering a wound in the flank from one of the curved tusks. The dog's tough hide held scars from worse encounters, still I worried about the bleeding and possible infection.

We returned to the village with fresh meat, avoiding the water-hole on the way. Dusk gently moved through the valley. One of Togom's wives met us and hurried us into his hut. The wise men of Togom's age group who served as a village council sat cramped and cross-legged around a freshly lit fire.

Room was made for Togom, Ruta and myself. The warm, moist smell of unbathed humans who had labored through a hot afternoon was stronger than the smoky odor.

I held a strange position in village life and politics. I am White, child, female. According to Nandi laws, these should have excluded me from the circle. Yet there seemed to be a rule that said uniqueness exempts one from the rules. I was accepted because of my differences. So, as I had done before, I sat with the old men.

"While you were hunting, *ol-oiboni*, a magistrate came from Nairobi," one of them explained intensely. "With him were two *askari* who did not look like *askari*. They were natives, true, but they behaved like mongrel dogs, not like police officers. Our young men must go into the militia, the magistrate said. He strutted through the village as if he had a right to be here and bothered the young men, even the uncircumcised boys, for their names and the names of their brothers. He will be back, he said, with many more *askari* to take the young men away, even if they do not want to go."

"I will go to this war," said the youngest of the old men— for sometimes in the village old had nothing to do with years—still full of uncooled fire. "I will show the bravery of the Nandi *murani*." He shook a fist as if it held a spear.

"Aiyee," Togom said, "this is not a war of spears. This is a war of weapons falling from the sky. It is no place for a true warrior. There is honour in a spear, in staring into the eyes of your enemy, in judging his character and acknowledging his bravery. There is no honour in bombs."

"What do you know of bombs?" he challenged.

Togom's face took on the glow of the new fire. His eyes transformed from the hard black of the warrior into the soft brown of the seer. He looked through the flames, through the earth to the world's core. "A great bomb has already fallen. Hate explodes from its depths. We feel the heat. Soon we will know the burning."

The old men made it law: No Nandi will fight in this war.

It was almost too dark to find my way home when the meeting ended. Togom walked with Orion and me up the valley slope to the top of the hill closest to our farm. I would have to hurry, and there was still my father's wrath to face.

Togom put a hand on my shoulder as he often did when he had something important to say, as if the weight of his hand paralleled the weight of his words. A rim of soft brown still circled his black eyes. He moved dreamily, and I wondered if the vision he had in the hut moved with him at the edge of his sight.

He blinked several times before focusing on my face. "Elisbet, you must call to the animals. Tell them, do not go south, do not go west, do not go north. You must say, come to this valley. Kill only for food, not for territory. And do not kill until your hunger is very strong. The Nandi promise to do the same. Tell them, come close and be ready."

"Ready for what?" I asked, afraid he would tell me. My small, tired body trembled at the unknown image that circled his vision.

"Tell them."

Togom turned and walked unsteadily back toward the village. Limping from his wound, Orion did his best to guide me home in the closing darkness.

There is a human thing called a war that brings many dangers, I sent into the night to the animals. You must come to Njoro, to Rongai, because the *ol-oiboni* says it should be so. He sees many things that you and I cannot see. He knows many things that you and I cannot know. He thinks of many things that you and I cannot imagine. Come close so you will be ready.

That night in my little bed the village drums woke me. I was too exhausted from the day's hunt to decipher their meaning. Just as quickly the rhythm lulled me to sleep.

The next morning I sneaked out of my room and headed for the village to find out about the drums. I made Orion stay at the farm to give his injury time to heal. He scowled at me in his wide-jowled way but obeyed. The pain meant nothing to him, he told me.

I am not going hunting, I assured him. My knife and spear are only for protection.

He remembered charging the boar, Ruta's spear sticking from its back like a narrow third tusk. He remembered clamping his teeth into the boar's throat and shaking his head until the flesh tore and warm blood sprayed across his face. He did not remember the tusk ripping a gash across his flank. I am a better weapon than a knife and spear, he told me through his memories.

With longing, he remembered the lion at the water-hole, an opportunity missed because I held him back. You owe me a cat, he said.

Another time, dog, I told him with affection.

I took my usual path to the valley, reached the crest of the hill and looked down, eager to see the comforting domed roofs of the huts around the circular clearing, the wisps of smoke.

I saw nothing but the valley floor thick with foliage. My breathing came so fast I could scarcely draw oxygen from it and I thought I might faint. Tears blurred my sight. How could they leave? I thought, when I really meant How could they leave without me? How could they move a village and close plants over the spot where it had been so there was no sign it ever existed?

They couldn't, my mind shouted in disbelief. They couldn't leave without me—

They couldn't. Of course. So simple.

I hefted my spear and boldly walked into the valley as I always did, straight through the thick growth that should have swallowed me but didn't. As I descended, the surroundings blurred. I stepped, uncertain if my foot would find the earth. It settled on cleared ground despite what my eyes told me. I stepped again. Again.

The grass and leaves reformed into familiar patterns and opened a trail at my feet. Before me a village snapped into existence with the sudden sound of barking dogs and the smell of cooked boar from yesterday's hunt.

Ruta greeted me with a wide grin and twinkling eyes as if this was a joke meant just for me. "You have found us then, Elisbet. Our little trick did not fool you." Yet, obviously he knew that it had, at least for a little while, and he took some delight in that.

I tried to laugh through the rags of my fear. "So this is what you did with the drums making such noise all night so no one could sleep. You have made yourselves invisible."

He proudly pointed out the boundary of the illusion. "It is a small thing for an *ol-oiboni* as skilled as Togom," he said.

I followed the ripple that circled the village like a great ring of heat. It was not a small thing. Not a small thing at all.

Four days later open trucks rumbled along the road from Nairobi. I was at the edge of the farm exercising Valiant Lady, a golden beauty with more loyalty than legs. Her tendons were weak, and she required easy handling. She had been custom designed, the fertilized egg smuggled into Africa then implanted into our roan mare. Father forbid me to go hunting until my lessons were satisfactory, and he punished my disobedience by placing this wonderful creature in my care.

He said nothing of Finch's offer to take me to England; but nightly during supper while we discussed each horse's progress and possible training strategies, I knew he thought about it. Thought about sending me away. Away from him. Away from Africa.

The noisy trucks were empty, which meant they expected to pick up something to haul back to the capital. I followed the caravan, staying to high ground. The vehicles bumped onto the cart trail that twisted into the Rongai then stopped where Togom's illusion dissolved the road and barricaded the narrow entrance with phantom bamboo trees and thick vines.

A Black man dressed in blazing white shirt and shorts got out of the cab of the lead truck. He might as well have had MAGISTRATE stamped on him in bright letters. He fumbled with a map. The driver got out and pulled something with him. A large rifle, the kind for firing many bullets very quickly. Not a rifle to be used against animals but one to be used against humans. The man slung a strap over his shoulder to support the heavy gun. He strolled to the magistrate's side with an ease that said he was used to the extra weight and hardly knew how to walk without the additional appendage at his side.

I suspected that the men packed into the cabs of the other trucks also had such rifles and such walks.

The two studied the map for a long time. They poked fingers at it, gestured in confusion to the road and the hills. The gunman strolled a little way into the bush then returned, rubbing his temple as if it ached.

They came to take the young Nandi men, to train them as soldiers to fight in the war that had begun in the far south and that moved closer each day.

I watched them and knew that the war was already here.

The magistrate shouted orders. He and the gunman got back into the truck. Vegetation pushed as close to the trail as it dared, sometimes snaking over it with great bravado. There was no clearing large enough for a truck to turn around in. The entire caravan crawled backward along the cart trail like a segmented worm. The string of dust-caked vehicles had to back up all the way to the Nairobi road. And it would return to the capital empty.

I laughed, urging Valiant toward the farm. She shook her pure white mane and flicked her snowy tail ready to do anything I asked.

Two days later in the grey morning, Kitau stumbled onto the veranda, panting like an ill-used steeple chaser. He and some of the other workers took turns going to Nairobi so we had daily bulletins about the war.

Father and I were just about to go to the stables. Father, broad and beefy, supported the wiry Kitau and placed him in a chair. The young man's appearance with the sunrise spoke more eloquently of horror than his words ever could.

"*Bwana* and *Memsahib* Kreshenko," Kitau puffed out between gulps of air, "murdered." He glanced at me then quickly returned his water-smoothed stone eyes to my father. "And their little ones with them."

I was only eight, but I knew both masks death wore, the natural and the tragic. I felt more rage at the injustice of murder than sorrow at the loss of the Kreshenkos.

Violence had moved north blindly. The animals' increasing distress had become an expanding roar in my head. Cats. Monkeys. Elephants. Rhinos. Zebras. They rushed like a stampeding zoo before the advancing guns and bombs.

Some had been caught in bursts of fighting that flared like spontaneous combustion.

Humans have gone mad, they told one another. Humans have gone mad.

Father put his hands on his hips. He shifted his mouth as if he chewed a piece of tough meat. "Who did it? Their servants?"

"No, no," Kitau protested. "You must not think such a thing. For the servants are dead beside their master and mistress. Much was burned. It is the police who believe that this and other things were done to hide the identity of the murderers. In front of their clerk the police say it was activists from South Africa who wish once again to form the Mau, so they can drive out all Whites. They say they know this from other police. *Bwana* Kreshenko and his family are not the only Whites to be killed. The police say this in front of their clerk and their clerk says this to me."

"You ran all night?" It seemed unfair that the Thoroughbreds in our stable rested comfortably while Kitau traveled from Nairobi to Njoro on foot. Father wanted the workers to take the horses, but they were experienced runners, not riders. They had more stamina, were more sure-footed in the uncertain terrain and needed less rest than the products of royal bloodlines who still slumbered in their boxes.

Kitau nodded.

"That's dangerous."

The Kikuyu silently told my father that it was necessary, and my father silently thanked him.

"The Haugens?"

"Gone quickly more than a day ago. The servants bring many boxes to the city to send after them."

"Any news of Finch and his wife?" my father asked carefully as if he suddenly had difficulty speaking.

"Safe. In Nairobi. That is the other message I bring. They leave tomorrow for England and say they would be most pleased to take little Elizabeth with them."

My world stopped. I closed my eyes, afraid to blink, afraid any movement would start time again and I would be on my way to Nairobi with a suitcase, wearing the dress from last Christmas that was too small for me but was the only one I owned.

My father looked at his boots. His shoulders lifted with the intake of a great breath then sagged with decision. "No." A long word that hung in the growing heat. "Lizzy belongs here. I'll send word to the Finchs. Kitau, get some food and rest. I'll have guards posted around the farm."

My world had movement and meaning again. I ran into my father's arms; they were suddenly low enough to catch me up and swing me to his chest. We held one another and let the horses wait.

That night snarls and screams woke me to the dark. At the foot of my bed raged a battle of teeth and claw. Orion and the red-maned lion.

I heard the lion carry the dog from the room in triumph. Heard Orion struggle and snap in the grasp of its jaws, taking away any dignity the lion had hoped for.

Sayid appeared with an electric torch, Father with the rifle that lately was never far from his hand. Together we followed a broken line of shiny blood while I followed Orion's anger.

I knew the dog twisted in the lion's jaws and was released. I knew he rolled then gained his feet and faced the glittering eyes. To Orion's credit, he didn't challenge the lion's right to sneak into the house if it could, nor to enter my bedroom if it went undetected, nor to grab a sleeping dog and make off if nothing stopped it.

With bleeding pride Orion stared at the lion. He had not smelled the lion, not wakened to the soft padding of its paws as it entered the house or the little bedroom. He was humiliated by being snatched up in his sleep then dropped in the dust. He barked fiercely, demanding a rematch.

We reached the animals, a composite of light and shadow in the beams of our torches. I ordered Orion into silence and was surprised when he obeyed.

The red-maned lion stood calmly. Scarlet dripped from the wounds Orion had managed to inflict.

My father pressed his torch into my hand. Slowly he raised the rifle to his shoulder.

Why did you do this? I asked. No reply.

"It's not going to charge," I whispered. Togom's training told me, not anything I heard.

Before I finished the words, the cat melted into the night.

The next morning I forced a sulking Orion to stay at the farm while I disobeyed my father and went to the village. The dog's neck was torn open in many places from the lion's teeth, but most of the wounds were not deep.

I had seen what a lion could do, what the red-maned lion had done when its purpose was death. It had not dragged off Orion in order to slay him. It had not taken him because he was a fierce dog who killed cats for the challenge. That was Orion's right as a hunter. The lion had another purpose. I was a child and wished I had Togom's wisdom so I could understand.

"The lion would not tell me why," I complained to Togom after telling of the attack. The *ol-oiboni* and I shared a breakfast of fruit and flat bread baked from flour Father had sent some time ago as a present.

Togom sat cross-legged and rocked slightly in thought. "Perhaps the lion is saying, 'I do not like what is happening. I do not like what these human animals do.'"

"Then why didn't it just tell me instead of hurting poor Orion?"

"Perhaps the message was not for you." He rocked and pursed his lips. His hard eyes grew soft at the edges. "I will think many things about this, Elisbet. I will think like a lion, then the meaning will come to my mind."

I didn't go hunting that day. I followed my own trail back to the farm to nurse Orion.

A battered blue truck sat in the bare space before the house. It was an ancient, wasteful vehicle without a fluid unit to store energy when it idled or went downhill. The official seal on the door was unreadable through the thick coating of reddish dust, but it must belong to a Nairobi magistrate. No other official would come to Njoro.

A Black man, tall and thin as most natives with the sculptured features of the Kamba tribe, stalked from the house, a piece of paper clenched in his hand. He folded himself into the truck, and it took him away with much chugging and complaining.

My father stepped onto the veranda. His boots made solid clomps on the cedar boards. He put his hands on his hips and watched the dust plume grow thin.

I came up beside him. Although he didn't look at me, he knew I was there. I slipped my hand through the triangle his arm made and placed my small fingers on the back of his hand.

"They can't order me off my own land," he said softly. The more angry my father was, the lower he spoke. The quiet of his words made me shiver. "I chose this country and earned my keep. I've no intention of leaving."

Sayid was at his other elbow. "What will we do, *Bwana* Burton?"

My father, Sayid, and myself. Whenever I think of the old Africa, my memories are always of the three of us and the house as it used to be. I can close my eyes now and feel as I did at that moment with my hand touching my father's and the fragrance of curry that lived in Sayid's flowing clothes. This is the last of those memories.

"Pack my bag," my father told Sayid. "I'm going to Nairobi to straighten this out."

I didn't expect Father to come home that night. When he didn't return the second night, I could do little except sit on the veranda and watch the road until long after sunset.

Sayid tucked me into bed. Orion, much recovered and burning with the desire to kill a cat, took his usual place on the rug. The guards Father posted patrolled the immediate grounds of the house and stable. The red-maned lion roared just before I fell asleep.

Sayid woke me by the light of a small torch. I reached for the lamp switch, but he grabbed my hand. "There are headlights on the road," he said. "They do not belong to your father's truck." I couldn't tell if his hand shook or if it was mine wrapped in his that quivered.

My knife and spear lay in the rippled folds of my covers, placed there by Sayid.

"Go to the village," he said. "Not to worry. They are only government officials come to make you leave. I will tell them *Bwana* Burton went to Nairobi two days ago and has not returned, for that is the truth. And if they know that a daughter lives here also, I will say that little Elizabeth went to England with *Bwana* and *Memsahib* Finch. If they search your room, I will say you took little because these things are not what young girls wear in England, and these things are not what young girls play with in England."

His quick cadence told me it was a well-rehearsed speech, something he and Father prepared before Father left.

In a sharp flash I heard the approaching intruders. Their thoughts were simple and loud. They had not come from the government at Nairobi to enforce an evacuation of the White farmers. They came only to destroy.

I gripped Sayid's sleeve with my free hand. "Order the horses released, and the chickens. Send everyone away. You must go too."

Sayid looked deeply at me. In the torch's glow his face was round shadows and curved dark skin. He seemed relieved that I knew what he tried to hide from me, that we parted without a lie between us, even one meant in kindness. I hugged him completely and forever.

I dressed quickly and took up my weapons. Then I opened the door to my chameleon cage and left, warning Orion to be quiet. I went as far from the farm as the dog could lead me in the dark. I heard the confusion of the horses as they were turned out into the night. There is danger here, I told them and the other animals. I flee from it myself. Move quietly, now, away from this place.

I stopped to wait for the almost full moon to rise higher, so I could find my way to the village by its light. From my hiding place I watched the farm.

Four Jeeps roared like blind elephants into the yard and abruptly halted. The headlights turned movement into a grotesque dance. The shadows of men jumped from the Jeeps.

They fired guns into the air, large guns, the kind carried by the man with the magistrate. I buried my face in Orion's scarred coat and held him fiercely to me.

A growing brightness came too soon and harsh to be the gentle moon. The stable glowed then exploded in heat. Flames waved like wheat stalks. The house burned with the reflection; the reflection became flames. Timbers crackled, cracked and fell. I heard rifle shots but could not guess what they meant.

From an adjoining hill the roar of the red-maned lion shook the earth. I watched until the slanted roof over the veranda crumbled to meet the cedar boards. *"Kwaheri,"* I told Njoro. Farewell.

The moonlight was soft. I blinked until the images of flames dissolved, then crossed over the hill into the valley. I passed through the blurry illusion that surrounded the village, barely aware of the distortion.

In the center of the circle formed by the huts stood Togom. Moonlight spread from him and filled the village. Beside him stood a man and a woman I did not know. The man seemed older than Togom, wrinkled like a dried creek bed, hair greyed to a cloud of white. The woman was smooth-skinned. At the focal point of what must be a ceremony, she was composed beyond her youth.

The villagers sat in the worn dirt, forming a thick moat of dark water around the island of soft light occupied by Togom and his companions. But there were far more people than this village usually held, and there were many faces I did not recognize.

Togom held out his hands to me across the moonlight and gestured. Waves passed through the water and a path opened. I walked through to the center, Orion at my heels. The dog held his head high, aware that there was honour in this. I took my clues from him and from the young woman beside Togom. I would not let the sorrow of Njoro that cried out for comfort mar my behavior.

"*Koaribu*," come you are welcome, Togom said. "We have been waiting for you, Elisbet. Maina," he gestured to the old man, "has brought his people. And Jebbta," he moved a hand toward the young woman, "has brought her father's people that we might unite the power of the Nandi against this war that has no honour."

I entered the island of light and stood with the straight posture of a *muran*.

Togom spoke to the valley. "In the timeless past the Nandi walked Africa, moving as the hunt and grazing land for our cattle took us. But the government of Whites and the government of Blacks who had given up their tribes told us we must live on only one part of the land, that only certain places in Africa were ours and only the game on that land was ours and we must live by these laws."

The *ol-oiboni* gave a little smile. "To their eyes, we obeyed; but we are Nandi and will not be ruled by others." The smile dissolved into pain. "Now they invade the little plots of land they said were ours, with their bombs and their guns and their war. We must protect ourselves from their foolishness until Africa is again ours to walk as we will.

"Elisbet, call the animals into the Rongai. Say they must come over the top of the hills and onto the slopes that bend to the valley." Togom's eyes had grown soft, as if he dreamed. "Tell them that this is Africa now. Life and death hold equal honour here."

I listened. Panic echoed from the farm and from other places I could not identify.

Come, I called into the moonlight. It is not a child who calls to you but the noble Nandi. We invite you to this valley, to the land we have shared with you since before time. And we will hunt. And you will hunt. Here, all will be as it was.

Silence. Silence. Silence. My heart stopped beating.

The red-maned lion roared, accepting the bargain.

Leopards snarled, elephants trumpeted, zebras neighed. I covered my ears against the answers but I could not keep them out of my head. Nor did I want to.

Up in the hills the jungle rustled slightly with eland and impala as if no more than a breeze stirred. Under my feet the ground quivered. In my mind I heard animals crest the hill, heard the horses from the farm, heard the ones already in the valley adjust to make room.

They took positions watching the village. And waited.

I nodded to Togom, but he already knew.

Togom spoke to the humans and the animals. "What we do has not been done since before the birth of my father and his father and his father and more fathers before that. One *ol-oiboni* cannot accomplish it alone. This is why *ol-oiboni* Maina and his people have come. This is why Jebbta and her people have come. Jebbta's father is dead, killed by a bomb dropped from the sky. It is a bad way for a Nandi *muran* to die, and it is bad for an *ol-oiboni* to die so young without another ready. Jebbta takes his place tonight. Although female and not formally trained, she knows her father's work and she will do well."

The three formed a circle—arms outstretched, palms upward, fingertips touching. The moon floated above as if its light fell only on the Rongai.

The drums began a slow rhythm. The assembly seemed gently pulled to its feet. Ruta came forward and took my hand. He led me into the gathering of villagers and those newly arrived. With the others I swayed and danced to the drums.

Orion sat and watched the three immobile *ol-oiboni*, as if it were his duty to witness for his kind. But I knew what the dog did not. The red-maned lion stood in a moon-cast shadow on the nearest slope, *ol-oiboni* for the animals.

The moon slid behind a hill. The drums stopped in the darkness. Togom broke the circle and smiled tiredly, sadly at Maina and Jebbta. "The valley is sealed. The outside cannot see us, can no longer touch us. So it will be until the time arrives for us to take back what was once ours."

Togom carried me into his hut because I was too tired to make my own way. I dreamed of hot flames and cool moonlight and quivering earth.

In the morning the village was busy accommodating its new residents and setting up a system for handling the limited resources.

"Elisbet," Togom said, "you must help the animals establish territories that will keep them from arguing with one another. Their numbers must be balanced so every kind will survive."

I called Valiant Lady and the other horses to the village. They were beautiful and strong and very fast, but they didn't know how to protect themselves against cats and boars. I loved them so and was glad to stroke Valiant's silky coat.

Their lives were now changed as much as mine. They would be useful. There were many places they could not go because of the dense growth, but also many in the valley and up the steep hills where they could carry a rider. I didn't think beyond that. Not then. I didn't consider that their descendants would be useful to my descendants. But I think in such terms now.

I ride a three-year old stallion, one of Valiant's line, to the crest of the hill nearest where the farm used to be. The same hill I scrambled over in the moonlight with Orion nine years ago when I was eight. The dog slowed with age, and on one of his cat hunts he lost the battle. I have no interest in another dog.

I was such a small child, my father would be surprised to see how tall I have become. I am as long-legged and straight and graceful as any Nandi.

I stretch out a hand and touch the smooth, hard nothingness of the elongated bubble that separates the winding valley from the charred wasteland beyond. I stoke the ancient protection that Togom called up, as I call animals, from the depth of the Nandi heritage. It is not magic. It is something more solidly rooted in the earth and the rightness of things and the place where life began and will not let go.

I close my eyes and concentrate as hard as I can. I listen beyond the barrier, hoping.

Nothing.

I turn and gaze across the valley thick with green, noisy with life. A patch of moisture at the top of the otherwise invisible dome forms a cloud that will become rain.

Very close I feel the presence of the red-maned lion, although he doesn't speak to me. Old enough to be immortal, he often stalks the perimeter, as I do, to assure himself that it still stands and all is well.

Someday the descendants of the three *ol-oiboni* will open the bubble; and the Nandi will reclaim the wounded world, heal it with their own health. By then I will be dead for centuries.

No matter. Although at times I dream of more, of what used to be and what could have been, this is enough. This valley is my world.

This is my Africa.

Midnight Haiku

Weary eyelids droop.
No one guards you when you sleep.
So don't. Not ever.

152

Sleep-waker

"*Mbaisa sana*," terribly bad, Togom said in Swahili. He inspected the cultivated patches terracing the western hills that sloped up from the village. Overnight maize had spread from its own stone-edged plots to invade neighboring soil and choke out the young wheat.

Togom's dark, lean-muscled body flowed among the stalks, barely disturbing the wide leaves. Always he moved as a *muran*, a hunter of the Nandi tribe. I didn't follow him into the wheat patch. Instead I bent to the earth where the maize had been planted, where it had a right to be but was not content to stay. In the long shadows of the African morning, remnants of old, dried out stalks stuck from the ground amid new green growth. It was as if in a single night the crop had matured and reseeded the ground, with some of the seeds dropping across the stones into the wheat. I crushed a long-dead, papery brown leaf in my hand. "How can this be?" I asked Ruta who stood closest to me. We spoke mostly in Nandi, using Swahili, Kikuyu, even English, according to need.

"Am I *ol-oiboni* to know such things, Elisbet?" he countered, as if it were foolish for me to ask. In the early morning coolness, he wrapped his *shuka* under one arm of his naked body, slanted it across his back and chest and knotted it on the opposite shoulder. He was wider and rounder than most Nandi but quicker with a spear than any except Togom. "It is. That is all." He meant to take away my frown, but worry dwelled beneath his grin. I felt my stomach clench.

The pale tufts of silk hanging from the maturing ears were beginning to darken, a sign that the thick yellow seeds encased in leafy cocoons approached maturity. Togom ordered the maize patches cleared.

"All," he said. "All."

I was seventeen. I had known Togom, the village's *ol-oiboni*, spiritual leader, since my father brought me from England to Africa when I was four; and I had lived in his hut as if I were his daughter since the closing of the Rongai Valley nine years ago. That was longer than I had lived with my father. I had learned not to ask for explanations Togom was not ready to give.

It had taken the combined power of three *ol-oiboni* to create the metaphysical dome that sealed us from the rest of the world, protecting us from the war that had burned Africa, and probably other continents as well. Although wonderfully wise in the way of the earth, Togom could not have raised the barrier on his own. Two other leaders came to join him, bringing the people of their destroyed villages. The ritual was successful but left us with three times as many to shelter and feed.

We fought daily against imbalances among animals, plants and humans, against inconsistencies within ourselves.

Mostly we did well. But this sudden renegade maize thrust an imbalance into the equation.

Young girls wrapped the leaves tightly around the cobs and tied them shut with vines. Murani, the men from the village, hacked the cylinders free with long knives. Children carried armfuls down the slope and stacked them in the clearing of hard dirt ringed by thatched huts. Following the murani, women loosened the roots with digging sticks and pulled the stalks from the ground. The air thickened with the scent of rich soil.

Togom, Ruta, I, and a few trusted others worked carefully to clear maize from among the slim wheat. I was tall and long-legged as any Nandi muran. The corn tassels reached my elbows while the wheat barely touched my knees. Impossible, yet many things that were impossible elsewhere grew naturally from the Rongai. I was such a thing. I was White, English, female; yet even when a child, I sat in council with Togom's generation and hunted with the men.

Now I came swinging my knife behind Kini, one of Ruta's many daughters. She expertly bit off lengths of vine with her teeth and bound up the ears in quick flashes of her brown hands. She wore a skirt of impala skins that touched her ankles. Golden strands of silk stroked one of her naked breasts. My paleness needed more protection. I wore a cloth poncho-style shirt and loose pants of scraped lion hide that were useful for riding. I always wore a hat of woven grass over my light hair to shade my face from the equatorial sun.

"Elisbet," Togom called to me. "You must say to the animals, watch for plants such as these. Eat the leaves if you are hungry, but do not eat the seed heads. Say they must tell you if any are found. This is most important."

Sometimes I wished I could speak to people in my mind

the way I spoke to animals. I tried to read Togom's taunt features. They only told me that he feared the strange overnight spreading of the maize and worried that it also encroached on the natural vegetation. Considering the hardiness of the native plants, that seemed unlikely. The grasses and vines and bushes and trees fought for territory as fiercely as the beasts. They would not easily make way for an interloper. Still, a few kernels in the stomach of an antelope could be carried many miles then defecated onto fertile ground, and Togom—*muran, ol-oiboni,* respected by the red-maned lion who refused to speak to me—worried.

I opened my mind to the world inside the dome that protected us from the burned earth. Eland, impala, zebra, duiker, dikdik, kongoni—I gave them Togom's message, ignoring the cats and hyenas and other meat-eaters, who would not notice a new plant. I told the domesticated cattle and horses of the village, who grazed nearby. Some of them knew the image I placed in their minds from having visited the terraced fields. Tasty, they told me. We will watch.

I also told the smaller animals who eat grains. I don't know if they understood. Their minds are too quiet for me to hear. They would not be able to tell me if they found the plant I warned them about.

"How was your sleep last night, Elisbet?" Togom asked as we worked.

I shrugged. "The same." With every passing night I slept worse, always dreamless and hollow. Each morning I awoke less rested and more ravenously hungry, as if I had battled some strange beast through the darkness. During the day, I ate more than my share. I felt guilty but could do nothing about this perpetual emptiness.

"This is most good maize, Elisbet," Togom said to me. "You

must not think that it is not so. Do you remember when your father sent it to the village as a present?"

I nodded, used to the sudden change of direction in our conversations. I hacked off another ear with my knife and tossed the green cone to a waiting child. I was a child myself then, seven years old, already a three-year veteran of Africa. Father had scooped up a double handful of bright yellow kernels in his large hands and placed it on a bandana. Then he knotted the ends of the cloth together and handed me the bundle with instructions to take it to Togom.

The improvised sack surprised me with its weight. Father had worked years to perfect the genetically altered hybrid. He did not have enough seeds to fully plant our own newly cultivated fields, so he could have used the double handful himself; but he knew the grain would feed many Nandi. They were better at herding cattle than farming, and the maize almost raised itself. Besides, I think his pride required him to share.

I walked across the breath of the farm at Njoro, my dog Orion at my side. My father never worried when Orion was with me. As other parents provided teddy bears for their children to scare away pretend monsters, so my father had made Orion to protect me from real beasts. I knew nothing of the dog's mixed genetic heritage, nor did I care. He was brown and white and huge. He could bring down a wild boar with his strong jaws, and he hunted cats for sport. My constant companion, a voice always in my head, he loved me and I loved him and that's all any little girl needed to know.

In the distance Mount Kenya stood purple and white. At the equator the sky is close to the earth. I imagined the mountain smelled of snow and that it touched a dome encircling the world. Orion and I climbed over the hill that separated the farm from the Rongai Valley and descended into the village. The bundle shifted shape in my arms as if it held liquid or a thing alive.

On that day so long ago, I felt great joy at my father's accomplishment, great affection for him for sending the product of his hard work to my friends the Nandi, and very grown up to be entrusted with the valuable gift.

Now as I chopped and tossed and chopped and tossed, I destroyed the last thing besides myself that was of my father. "Perhaps the maize is too good," I told Togom. "Some morning we will wake up and discover it has swallowed the huts."

"Elisbet," he said, "before he went to another place, your father and I speak many times. You do not know this. He came here to the village when you were busy with your England books and your horses and your doing other things. That is why I respect your father. Other White men say to the Nandi and the Kikuyu and the Masai, you come to us, come to our city, come to our little rooms with corners and sit on chairs, then we will tell you what to do. Your father was not like this. He came to the village and we talk of many things. But mostly we talk of the young Elisbet. He tell me what I will soon tell you, but first I must tell you another thing.

"Long before this," he moved his arm in a wide arc above his head to indicate the enclosing bubble, "your father tell me of the war far to the south, that in a while it would stretch flames toward the Rongai. I tell him yes. The wind carries the heat and when the fire comes it will be most bad. Bad for all, but most bad for Whites because there are Blacks who cannot think beyond their hate. He say he knows this for he, too, can smell it coming from the South. Then he say Elisbet has no mother and only a father and this is not enough for when the fire comes. I say the village has young women. He can choose many wives and then Elisbet will have many mothers. I was joking yet I was not joking. Your father was most serious. He say Elisbet will need mothers and she will need more fathers as well.

"Here all are mother and father to all children, for we are all of the same blood. But you, Elisbet, and your father are from England. You are of the Nandi spirit but not of the Nandi blood. Many times before a hunt you have tasted the blood of the bull with Ruta and me and the other *murani*. You know this is a ritual of great importance. On that day, I and your father, we drink blood still warm from the bull's throat as if we share from our own bodies. From then I am also your father. My wives are your mothers. You are English blood. You are Nandi blood."

I knew it was true for Togom never lied. I had loved him as a father for a long time and felt a loss at having had the right to call him by that title but not knowing the right was mine. "You should have told me."

"I tell you now. And I have more to say."

But I ran off through the swaying maize and didn't stop until I was high enough to look down on the circular thatched roofs of the huts. Between two of the circles children tossed green cylinders onto a growing mound.

I do not know what happened to my father, my English father. I know only that he left the Njoro farm for Nairobi to try to convince the Kenyan government to let us stay on the land we had purchased with European dollars and built on and sweated over and called home for four years. Whites were being sent back to their native countries because somewhere far in southern Africa a war was going on between Blacks and Whites. I had been born in England, but I knew from the depth of my soul that Africa was my native land.

The day after Father left, the reborn Mau Mau raiders—their predecessors having terrorized the original European settlers—came to murder us and destroy the farm. I fled to the Nandi village, as Father planned I should. It was where I would have gone anyway. The people from two distant villages had arrived before me. In the light of the full moon Togom and the other *ol-oiboni*, Maina and Jebbta, performed the ritual that raised the dome.

I never saw Father again. I suppose he was killed somewhere on the red-clay road between Njoro and Nairobi. Perhaps everything was dead outside the bubble that protected the Rongai.

Something silent watched me through a lattice of bamboo. I had sprinted into the jungle without my spear and had only the long knife still in my hand for protection. I am *muran*, I arrogantly sent to the watcher. What coward steals after me?

From behind the khaki canes drifted cinnamon and gold, the red-maned lion. I could neither swallow nor breathe. In all the years we had shared this land, he had never so much as acknowledged my thought-voice. Now he answered me with his presence.

You are no coward, I sent to him as an apology, this I know. We are both hunters. We face each other with honour.

Old enough to be immortal, he locked me in a stare. You are not a hunter as I am a hunter, his golden eyes said. He gave a slow growl to put me in my place. Gracefully he turned his back to me as if I presented no danger, flicked his copper-tipped tail and vanished into the bamboo.

Dazed and embarrassed I returned to the village. The lion

had come to speak to me in his own way, and I had insulted him with false bravado.

A pair of dikdik sent me thoughts of broad, parrot-green leaves sprouting from a central shaft. I must puzzle out the reason for the lion's visit, but that would have to wait. I repeated Togom's message to the tiny antelope about what parts to eat and what not to eat. It is the *ol-oiboni* who says this, I reminded them as I hurried to find Togom.

The dikdik were unable to give me a precise location. They showed me a clump of wattle trees, grass laced with cobwebs still beaded with dew, and creeping vines bright with flowers.

"This could be many places," Togom said when I reported to him. "You must take one of your horses and search."

Although the uncircumcised boys tended them along with the cattle and although some of the braver villagers occasionally rode them, the horses were always referred to as mine.

The pampered purebreds I had brought with me from the farm had died years before. They had been raised for speed on groomed tracks and were unaccustomed to living in the open surrounded by jungle. They interbred and their descendants did better, except for Valiant Lady's line.

The genetically enhanced, fertilized egg that had grown to become Valiant had been smuggled into Africa, violating the laws of the country it came from, most of the ones it traveled through, and the one it ended up in. Her golden coat, white mane and white tale bred true, but she died young after birthing only twice. Her offspring died younger. Only one produced a foal in its short life. That last colt seemed to grow too fast, going from wobbly-legged new-born to sturdy filly overnight. In a blink her health deteriorated, and another of my father's great experiments ended.

I chose the muddy-coloured stallion, who was mostly of Arabian heritage. "I may be gone several days," I told Togom.

"You will return to the village to sleep."

I laughed, thinking how ragged my slumber had been lately. I was better off not trying to sleep at all. "I will climb into a tree for the night. The leopards will not bother me. I will not see them, but I will hear their stealthy thoughts and tell them I am a Nandi *muran*, not to be bothered." I did not have influence with the red-maned lion, but I knew I could bully the other cats.

The muscles in Togom's face bunched with rare anger. "And is the horse a *muran* feared by leopards? Can it climb a tree? Can it sit in the branches? No, you will return."

No more could be said.

After some wandering I found a cluster of maize in a setting just as the dikdik had pictured it. I tied up the immature ears and put them in a sack to take back to the village. Then I uprooted the stalks.

It was dusk when I returned. The children were snuggled together in the huts, and most of the adults as well. I sat on the hard ground in the village circle before the communal fire. The smoke was sharp with cedar. I listening to the night hunters and watching the stars through light clouds that clung to the top of the bubble. My eyes ached to close, but the dreamless half-sleep I dwelled in during the night was more exhausting than no sleep at all.

Togom sat down beside me and handed me a bowl made from a hollowed-out gourd. It sloshed with liquid. "Drink."

"What is it?" It smelled of bitter herbs and the deceptively sweet siafu plant. Named after the black warrior ants, siafu was medicine when weak and deadly poison when strong. One way or another it cured most illnesses.

"Drink."

"If we are to control the maize," I said, "I must ride all of the Rongai."

"Kimani again asks to marry you."

Ruta and I often chatted away about nothing and everything, but Togom only spoke to me of important things. "I am too old," I said. But I was not. Togom had urged the young people to wait extra years before marrying so their children would not strain the limited resources of the village. There were many unmarried girls with good prospects who were as old as I.

"And you are a funny looking European," Togom said, "who must hide her pale skin under strange clothing. Yet, Kimani wishes to set a dowry."

"He is ambitious and wants a tie to you because you are the spiritual leader."

"Yes. This is not a bad thing."

Firelight painted his eroded skin. His black eyes grew soft brown halos, and I wondered what vision formed in the flames. In this place the physical and the spiritual were weft and warp of the same fabric, so I didn't think it strange for my adopted father to slip into a trance. While I had gone the short step from child to adult since Togom and Maina and Jebbta placed the bubble over the valley, it seemed Togom had trudged a hundred years.

"Will he tell me I cannot hunt?" I challenged. "Will he tell me I cannot ride? Will he think I should only do the things his other wives do?"

"Perhaps."

"Then I will not marry him."

Togom gave a single nod. "That is what I have said to him."

It was a lesson then, to guide me to think about my future. "I will marry no one. And I will succeed you as *ol-oiboni.*" Today I learned he was a true father to me. I had a right to ask this of him. Maina was decades older than Togom with a successor already trained. Jebbta was only ten years older than I. Although not formally trained, she had succeeded her father out of necessity when he had died during the journey to our valley. They each had their own people to look after. When the valley opened, they would travel on to reestablish their own villages.

It had taken three *ol-oiboni* to raise the barrier. I suddenly wondered if it also required three to remove it.

"Elisbet, my daughter," Togom said, voice as misted as his eyes, "it cannot be."

My pride twisted and bled. For whatever reason, he did not think me worthy. All of the village's previous leaders had been Nandi, of course, but I did not believe it was because of my fair skin. All had been male. But since I had already done most things usually restricted to *murani,* I did not believe it was because of my gender. Togom was too wise to be distracted by such trivialities and too practical. He encouraged Jebbta to continue her studies. So his decision must be because of some flaw in me. I was not capable in some way.

The finality of his words made me wonder about what he saw in the flames—and about the contents of the bowl cradled in my hands. Wounded, I drank.

I don't know how I found my way back to the hut that night. I remembered nothing after drinking the potion until I saw light that was too sharp to be sunrise peaking around the edges of the worn blanket hung over the door. I squinted against the harshness, groggy although I had obviously slept late into the day. My tongue felt swollen and my head pulsed. Apparently for me the medicine was both poison and cure.

I craved water. Unsteadily I stood and took a step. I tripped over something and thudded to the dirt floor. I forced my eyes open. The fire in the center of the single room had burned to cold ash. Around it lay Togom's wives and children, his widowed sister and her two babies. I crawled to Wanjui, the youngest wife, and placed a hand under her nostrils. A slight breath brushed my palm. It seemed insufficient to sustain life. Her cheek was cool, but not cold, to my touch. I checked two of the others. They slept close to death, alive yet not alive.

This was too terrible to be real, so it must be a dream caused by the herbs and siafu extract. I stumbled from the hut into the village circle. Green stalks surrounded me. Disturbed by my sudden intrusion, tassels bobbed and swayed, stroking my shoulders. Maize flooded the ring, flowed between the huts and climbed up into the jungle.

Togom's head floated on the broad leaves. I waded through the thick sea to join him. He stood naked. He bound up cobs, hacked them loose and dropped them into a sling he had fashioned from his *shuka*. The stalks whispered my approach, but he did not look up from his work. "We were careless," he said. "Seeds escaped us and burrowed into the packed ground and now it is a field."

"This is not real," I told him. "When I wake, it will be gone."

He gave a great sigh. "The potion did not work."

"It gave me this dream," I said.

He looked centuries wearier than yesterday. "The others dream. But not you, Elisbet, and, for this time, not me. I have much work to do and you are not able."

I swept my mind across the hills, to the red-clay water hole, deep into the crevices of the Rongai. "It cannot be day. I hear no animals."

"Do you hear the leopard? Do you hear the night hunters?"

"I hear—" My head was empty, empty of everything except my own thoughts. Always, always there had been the voices of animals and the faint murmur of humans.   Now there was—"nothing."

"They sleep."

"Like Wanjui and the others."

"Yes."

"This is *ol-oiboni* magic," I said although I knew magic did not exist. Togom drew up the ancient spirit of the land and kept it close to life, that was all.

He shrugged. "I know what others do not know. I do what others cannot do. This thing has been done many times, but you do not know this. Many times sleep has been put on a place so it can wait."

"Wait for what?"

"What needs to happen," he said as if I should have figured that out. "The world was burned with strong fire. It needs time to heal. So we must wait. The valley goes to sleep at night and when it wakes, for the valley, it is tomorrow. But during this sleep many sunrises surprise the earth and coax it to grow, many nights cool it with rest."

"How many? For one day here, how many outside?"

"A year and a day." His eyes twinkled as if the extra day was a little joke. "To keep us even with the season."

The hot sun sent a trickle of sweat down my spine. I wished I had my hat. I did the math, not wanting to believe the result. I had not meticulously kept track of the days. Still, an estimate gave me over 3,300 years, thirty-three centuries.

"I am asleep and dreaming this, so it is not true; or I am awake and I should not be, so it is not true."

"We should be asleep. You and I and the maize. The maize sleeps very little no matter what I do. Less and less as each Rongai day passes. It plants itself and grows and drops seeds. The jungle is still, so the other plants do not take the moisture and the sunlight from the maize, they do not push it aside even in the thickest parts. During the passing of ninety-eight outside days, I cleared many places to the south and I thought I had beaten it. But while I was away from the village, the clever maize played a trick on me." He held out his arm and made a circling motion to encompass the green sea.

I envisioned the maize invading the huts, growing from the roofs and walls, smothering the sleepers inside. "Wake everyone," I cried. "Wake the jungle. In two days, three days, we can get rid of the maize."

"Aiyee, this is not like a blocked stream, Elisbet. I cannot remove the stones, let out a trickle of water, then place the stones back where they were. I can change nothing until the end of this cycle when the next Rongai day comes. That is a long time from now."

We cleared the village together, working through the silent sunrises and sunsets that touched the valley without affecting it. When we finished, Togom walked the valley floor where the vegetation was almost too thick for a man to pass while I walked the high hills. I zigzagged through the yellow-spiked cassias and large-petaled wild flowers that I now knew had held their fresh blooms for centuries. I climbed trees to scout the great open areas. No birds called, no eland thought of chewing soft leaves, no boar longed for cool water. Their silent spirits haunted the land. Always before now, the voices of animals had drifted through me like constant companions.

Now there was only the whisper of grasses against my legs, almost imperceptible for I moved with a quiet confidence firmly rooted in my training. For the first time I felt truly alone although I knew I was not. I lived inside this world as it lived inside me—every creature, no matter how small its voice; every human, no matter how unreadable the thoughts; every plant, although voiceless to my mind. Why was I awake? How could I be so joined and yet so separate?

My serpentine path took me many times to the bubble. I preferred to camp under greenery, but one dusk found me by the invisible barrier too exhausted and fearful of missing a patch of maize in the fading light to move inward. I turned my back to the charred, colourless land beyond the dome and curled up on the ground without concern for leopards. As I fell into the slumber of the outside world, I wondered again, why I did not sleep with the Rongai like the others.

I woke facing the black scape. New light reached a long hand to touch me, but that was not why I stirred. Something small and far away thought of hunger, of sweet leaves and tender branches to cure the ache. Something outside. I placed a cautious hand against the transparent barrier and stared into the distance. Did I see the tiniest fleck of green at the horizon or did I imagine it? No matter. I did not imagine the animal voice. I opened my mind wide. There were others now as the sun rose higher and dipped light into their hollow.

What beast are you? I asked.

We are we. We have hunger. We search for food. We stay near water.

I smelled fresh moisture and tasted liquid as pure as the stream that served the village. They had no name for themselves, since names came from humans and they had no knowledge of the pictures I put in their minds of Nandi and Masai and Kikuyu and Whites. Clear thoughts have nothing to do with animal type. Cats of all kinds are easily understood. The red-maned lion hears me and could speak back but refuses to do so. The gazelle has such small thoughts that it is unintelligible, while its cousin the eland has a quick, precise voice that is hard to miss. From the misty images these new creatures sent, I could tell only that they lived on land and survived on sparse vegetation.

As I went about my task, I listened in the otherwise silent day, glad to have the soft thoughts with me. I found a patch of immature stalks among sweet potatoes. The feathery plants sucked moisture away from the vines so even in a dormant state the purple flowers hung limp. I began pulling the stalks from the heavy soil and scattering them where they would decay and join the cycle of the valley instead of disrupting it.

My father's maize. He had labored over the golden kernels while we were still in England, and he dreamed of Kenya despite those who tried to wake him to their definition of reality. He tried many crossed varieties, many genetic alterations. When he finally established the farm in Africa and sowed the seeds he had carefully smuggled past quarantine, they failed. So did others after that. I remember his joy when this incarnation defiantly survived to maturity, suffering minimal damage from diseases and weevils and drought that seemed to defeat everything except the native plants and the few coffee bushes remaining from the first European settlers.

Now the maize thrived here, but it was not part of the rhythm of the land.

The faraway animals startled and hid at the approach of

something not of their kind. I felt meat-hunger. The hunter smelled spoor, peered through a curtain of rushes, plotted a stealthy path to its prey. Its thoughts were familiar yet strange. It was no kind of cat I recognized. What are you? I asked, but it heard nothing through its need.

I ached to see these creatures who saved me from total aloneness. Of what variety were they? How had they survived the fire that seemed to have consumed the earth?

The weight of a sudden realization pushed me to my knees. How slow I was. How asleep my brain while my body walked!

Outside there were plants, animals who ate plants, animals who ate animals. The valley did not have to sleep. It could be opened. Then the maize would be controlled by the natural vegetation. I would not grow old while the others moved ageless in slow motion through time. Blackness still ruled beyond the bubble, but a spot of green sparkled like a gem at the horizon. At least I thought it did. I couldn't be sure.

I finished stripping out the maize, for something in me could not leave the task incomplete. Then I set off at a hunter's run. In the Rongai there are no straight paths. I worked my way toward the lip of the valley. "*Ol-oiboni*, " I cried with my voice and my mind. Most of the time I cannot understand the thoughts of people. They usually think of many things at once and I cannot tell where they focus. Only simple motivations are obvious to me. Togom was complex. I often did not understand what he said, so there was no hope I could decipher his thoughts. But perhaps he could send me an image.

Many minds shimmered with sleep. One mind swirled like a bright pool. I laughed as I followed the line of the Mau Forest then dipped down along a path I knew, understanding the message.

Togom rested under a rock canape beside the water hole, dark body merged with the shadow of the overhang. The marks of hooves and paws pocked the surrounding red clay. On sleepless days eland and zebra and impala came to drink with ears and eyes alert for predators. The red-maned lion prowled here often. Perhaps he slept just beyond the tall grass. He would not mind Togom's being here, for Togom is an honoured hunter like himself. But he would frown at me, especially after I insulted him that day in the bamboo.

Breathless, more from excitement than running, I gasped out what I knew, what I suspected, what I hoped. Togom considered it with a stony face. I studied his disappointing calm.

"It is not that I doubt what you sense, Elisbet, but only your belief of what it means. I must think of it."

And he would say no more.

For months we fought the maize. I traveled the elevations and depressions of my world, alone except for distant animal voices. There were not many kinds of them and not many of each kind. Mostly they were hungry and afraid to leave their water supply. The spring seemed to be their only guarantee of life. During the past years, I had considered nothing beyond the Rongai. Even when I imagined that my father might still be alive, I did not think of him forced to return to England without me or in Nairobi or at what had once been our farm. Instead I see him here, strolling into the Nandi village, a big man with a strong step who would swing me up into his arms as always. Silly, I know.

On the appointed evening I met Togom in the village. We settled into our usual places in his hut among his slumbering wives and children. I remembered folk tales of sleeping towns and castles. For the first time I considered that truth dwelled behind them.

In the morning, the Rongai morning, the rustle of life brought a comfort I had not felt for a long time. Togom had me send the animals searching into the thicker growth and less accessible rocky slopes for the enemy maize. "You must remind them not to eat of the seed. The young ones forget easily."

Wild goats reported broad-leaved sprouts. A swaying line of young girls walked off singing to uproot them.

Togom's eldest wife organized the women to grind up the kernels from the many ripe cones. The pile had more than doubled with the addition of what Togom and I had collected during our year. No one asked how the bounty had suddenly multiplied. Perhaps they thought the *ol-oiboni* had brought it down from the clouds during the past night and dried it with a spell-cast wind.

The women worked stone on stone. I inspected the flour, plucking out kernels that slipped by and putting them back into the bowls of unground grain. I instructed the older girls to do the same.

Kini watched me from the shade of lowered eyelids. "Yesterday we were of the same height," she said almost in a whisper. "Yesterday you did not have such a mark." She pointed to my hand where a red line stretched from knuckle to wrist. The scratch from a thorn was now almost healed.

We had played together, sung together, danced together, hollowed nut casings for ornaments together. In her yesterday we had been the same age. Now I was a year older. In her tomorrow I would be a year older still. She would watch me shrivel and die in months. I would never celebrate her wedding or be favored aunt to her children as we had planned.

I had no words to explain, so I said nothing.

The village slept the normal sleep of a normal night. For a few more hours they breathed in unison with the outside world. Togom, Ruta and I sat at the communal fire. Hyenas and leopards scouted the hills. The red-maned lion roared a greeting to the rising moon then roared again.

"He does not like the sleep you place on him, Togom," Ruta said, rolling a hollow clay oval in his hands. The maize kernels sealed inside chanted swish, swish, swish.

I was not surprised that Ruta knew about Togom's spell. "Perhaps when he showed himself to me that is what he wanted to say, so I would say it to Togom."

"Elisbet, you did not tell me *simba* sought you out," Togom said.

"I tell you this now," I said. Ruta laughed for this was usually what Togom said to me when I asked him why he had kept something from me for so long. "To this lion, I am only a lowly messenger."

"Do not be quick to say so," Togom said. "This you must think on."

"You have time to think about the whole world," Ruta said. "The maize will no longer bother us. We have flour to last many meals and we have seeds for when they are needed." Swish, swish, swish, he rolled the clay. "It is funny, Elisbet. Seeds inside an egg." He tossed the ball at me through leaping flames. I snatched it from the air. He gestured to the sky. "Seeds inside an egg."

"When will you open this egg?" I asked Togom.

"I will know when it is time."

"There are animals," I said.

"Are they animals like we know or are they something else born of the fire? You do not know this. I do not know this.

Your beasts might be very far away, perhaps as far as England."

I put the oval on the ground and watched firelight dance on the smooth surface. Something in me needed more although I realized the outcome would be the same.

"The outside is black, no colour," Togom said, responding to my unvoiced skepticism. "No birds have touched the outside sky, Elisbet. The land grows nothing. It is not enough for the land to be ready to accept the seed. The seed must also be ready to accept the land."

"Always one brave seed goes before the others," Ruta said. Togom gave him a heavy look. Ruta stood, knowing he had been dismissed by Togom the *ol-oiboni*, not Togom his friend. He grinned, circled the fire so he could ruffle my short hair, then sauntered with an enviable grace toward his hut.

"Will you sleep now?" I asked Togom.

"What would you have me do?"

I wanted to shout, stay awake with me! Roam the slumbering Rongai with me so I will not be lonely. Togom was already an old man. How many years before he died? Who would protect and guide the village then? "Sleep," I said. "A year is not such a long time." But I knew it would be an eternity. "Leave me a horse." I tried not to whine like a beggar.

"Ah, if I could do this, Elisbet, I would have kept Ruta and others awake to hunt the maize. I would give the red-maned lion his wish. But I cannot. I can only keep myself outside the blanket because I am the weaver."

I realized I had been avoiding the question I most needed an answer to. "Togom. Father. Why do I not sleep?"

Togom nodded. Often during our conversations I felt that he was waiting for me to ask the right question. "Your

England father gave the village this maize, which is good maize but not like the plants we know. And your father gave you Orion, which was a good dog but not like the dogs of the village."

There were no words to describe genetic engineering in any of the tribal languages we intermixed. And he would not understand the meaning behind the English ones. "Not natural," I offered.

Togom shrugged. "What is natural? I am *ol-oiboni*. Many things that I do are not what others do; yet these things are of the earth, they are of the long past and the present and the future. They are of the Nandi and the Rongai and Kenya and Africa. Your father was White yet he was *ol-oiboni*. That is why he came here, Elisbet, where the land reaches to the sky and cuts deep to the heart of the world. What he made was of this place, yet he was of far away and so it was not of this place.

"At first after Maina and Jebbta and I performed the old, old ritual, all slept; but this did not continue. For Orion, the spell became a pond that sends mist into the air and goes gradually dry. Although he tried so he would not leave you, Elisbet, he could not stay submerged."

"Orion?" I remembered patches of gray in his fur that grew larger from day to day. "Dogs do not live as long as people. But he did not die of old age as he would have if he had stayed awake all those years. He was killed by a cat he hunted."

"His legs slowed. His jaws were not so strong. He says to himself, I am *muran* and I will die as *muran*. This was of his own choosing."

My wonderful Orion, the companion of my childhood, never far from my side, he had suffered the aloneness. I thought of scars that had appeared on his hide overnight. I had accepted his excuses instead of demanding explanations.

"Why did you not tell me?"

"I tell you now," Togom said. "And I say to you what your father said to me. Elisbet is like Orion. Elisbet is like the maize. She was made as they were made."

I sat for a long time, blocking the realization that struck like lightning, but I could not stay numb. "And like Valiant Lady," I said. "Genetically engineered. Not natural."

Across the fire Togom sat cross-legged and silent while the wood burned to iridescent embers. Then he went to his hut to sleep, but I did not.

For a year I paced the valley, avoiding the village except to replenish my food sack. The huts seemed haunted by my friends and adopted relatives who slept as dead.

I told myself I searched to root out invading maize and keep the valley safe. I was a heroic guardian with a purpose. But I found no maize. From the beginning I knew it was a poor lie and I did not believe it for very long.

Outside the dome the wind whirled the ashes of my old world in circles. Rain washed the great inverted bowl, draping it in watery curtains. The sun rose and set. The moon rose and set. Inside I walked through frozen time. The only changes were from my actions—the fires I built, the branches I bent, the grass I crushed, the motionless boars I killed when I craved meat. At first I tried to make no mark, as if I had no right to score this place. Then I made many if only to later discover signs of myself. All the while, I conversed with the animals beyond the barrier.

In the early morning of the village's next day I waited in the dark for Togom to emerge from his hut. Creatures stirred with small thoughts. Close, very close, the red-maned lion roared.

"Ah, Elisbet," Ruta greeted me, "*na furie sana ku wanna na wewe.*" I am very happy to see you again, although for him it had been only last night that we spoke by the fire. "Togom," he called. The sound of a human voice was strange. "Elisbet seems most eager for you to come out."

Togom appeared, wrapping his *shuka* around the waist. "Today I will go hunting," I boldly told him.

A storm formed in his eyes as he understood my meaning. "Aiyee, you are like Orion, Elisbet, but you are not like Orion."

"I will drink the blood of the bull and track the red-maned lion. Now he will listen to me. Now he will answer me."

"Perhaps this is so," Togom said. "Perhaps not."

"It is so." I needed it to be so.

"Perhaps you will do something else," Ruta said.

"There is nothing," I said.

"The animals in the other world, what do they tell you?" Ruta asked.

I wanted to ignore what seemed a diversion, but Ruta locked an arm around me and gave me a good-natured squeeze so that I had to answer. "Mostly they are hungry."

"Do they eat maize?" he asked.

"They could but they have none."

"This is a pity," Ruta said. "We have maize we dare not grow. They have no maize and starve."

"There is nothing that can be done," I said, "and now I will go hunting."

"No hunting today." Togom made a chopping motion with his hand, ending the issue without discussion.

I would forego the blood ritual, then, and go directly to the lion. It suddenly occurred to me that he had thought of this first, as a solution to his own discontent. Mentally I called a challenge to him. Is this what you wanted of me, I asked him, when you stalked me at the bamboo?

Nothing. He was as stubborn as my Nandi father.

Though no one saw the beast, that day his paw prints appeared in the soft earth at the edge of the grazing land; and throughout the village night, while the others slept a true sleep before the spell-cast one, I heard his low snarls roll across the surrounding hills.

This time I took a great quantity of food with me. I counted the days only so I could pace my journey along the perimeter. A quarter of the oval in one fourth of a year. Halfway around in half a year. As the Earth orbited the sun, I orbited the village. During the days I quizzed the far off, unseen animals about their lives. Nights I spent sleeping under trees heavy with the dark fruit of leopards.

I often considered taking my own life with a wound or by hanging. But these were only exercises for an idle mind. That was not how I lived. Togom and Ruta—and I—would be disappointed in such a passive escape, and Togom would not allow me Orion's. I often stared at the blackened landscape outside the barrier and wondered if another exit from this limbo existed.

The air was stale by the end of the year and the dawn of the Rongai day. With deep breaths the lush vegetation quickly revitalized it. Rain fell from clouds that skittered along the curved roof.

When I walked into the village, children I had held and fed and told stories to in their yesterday fled from my wild look. My hair was a year longer, my clothes a year more tattered, my mind a year crazier.

Yet, I felt a clarity.

"Ah, Elisbet," Togom greeted me. He looked refreshed and at ease.

"I have learned the question you're waiting for me to ask," I said.

"It has taken you so long and yet so little time."

"Can the bubble be opened a small bit, large enough for a person and a horse and a clay egg filled with maize?"

He frowned, gazed at the ground and slowly shook his head, not in answer but in reaction. I had asked the wrong thing, or asked it the wrong way. Animals stretched in the slow sunrise. A strong, familiar roar echoed across the hills.

"And also large enough for the red-maned lion," I said.

Togom raised his deep, unfathomable eyes to me. "This is a good thing, Elisbet. I will do this for you, my daughter."

The red-maned lion flicks his cinnamon tail as he strolls the blackened landscape. After two days of travel he still will not speak to me in my mind. I understand that I must learn to interpret his movements, to speak the language of lion, as Togom does. Beside him I ride the muddy-coloured stallion. In my pack clay eggs swish, swish, swish with maize. After the many shades of green in the Rongai the charred ground seems featureless. The emerald gem I may have seen at the horizon still eludes me.

I think, as I often have, of the crayon drawings I made as a child. Every hue I owned was scribbled into thick patches on a page then covered over with black. I would scratch a picture through the dark wax, revealing the astonishing colours beneath. This is how Africa has always been, deep with surprise.

For now, we are the only variation here. I lead us toward the voices of the far away animals. I have not allowed myself to miss Orion in a long time, but I miss him now. He would be angry with me for having a cat at my side. Orion was a great hater of cats, except as prey. We travel long days, having little interest in sleep of any kind. We want to be awake when our Africa again shows its colours.

Credits and Notes

"Folds of Blue Silk" copyright © 1993 by Danith McPherson

The story was originally published in *Amazing Stories*, May 1993.

The idea grew from a report on savant syndrome that was broadcast over public radio. I'd been reading about autism and having discussions with those more knowledgeable than I about the current research. At the same time a lot was happening concerning the rights of people who are viewed as handicapped. Because the main character's mind functions differently from the norm, the story had to be told in her voice, and in the present tense.

"Jonah." copyright © 2019 by Danith McPherson

"Jonah" was written as a challenge at a writing workshop. Tell a story in fifty words.

"The Universe Seen as a Floating Orange Rind" copyright © 1989 by Danith McPherson

This story first appeared in *Space and Time*, issue #76, Summer 1989.

I've always enjoyed the way Shakespeare played around with mistaken identities. What would you do if strangers acted as if they knew you and as if you'd done things you were certain you never had? This story is my foray into that disorienting world. Plus an alien!

"Pleiades" copyright © 2019 by Danith McPherson
    The Pleiades star cluster is a favorite of mine. You can see it with the naked eye, but it is better through binoculars and best through a telescope. Although it is also known as the Seven Sisters, there are far more than seven stars in the cluster.

"Litany for Lost Heroes" copyright © 2019 by Danith McPherson
    I was thinking about how quick humans are to label beings as "alien" and "other," even when they're much like us. Even when they are us. People get lost in that kind of world.

"Attic." copyright © 2019 by Danith McPherson
    This is my ode to all the things in my head that I can't let go of, even when I know I should.

"Shifting Spirits" copyright © 2019 by Danith McPherson
    The discussions about climate change seem to be missing an important component: As a living part of the environment, humans are affected by it as much as migrating birds and hungry polar bears. Maybe it will cause us to lose our souls. Literally.

"The Night Lives Immense" copyright © 1991 by Danith

McPherson

This poem was originally published in *Sozoryoku*, issue #4, 1991.

The images came out of my interest in astronomy. I am an untrained amateur, and view the night sky more from an artistic perspective than a scientific one.

The story was first published in the anthology *Full Spectrum 4* in 1993. I was ecstatic when it was then selected for inclusion in *The Year's Best Fantasy and Horror, Seventh Annual Collection.*

"Roar" has been referred to as magical realism. I didn't write it with that intent, but I can accept that description. I don't think of anything in it as magic. Instead, what happens is the manipulation of nature using a specific kind of science. To me, the tale is an alternate history. I'd been reading non-fiction about coffee plantations and racehorse ranches owned by European colonists in Kenya before the Mau Mau Rebellion. I was fascinated by the mix of people, the scope of the landscape, and all that comes with it. Despite the vastness, it felt isolated and insulated. I envisioned a future version of that world. If humankind can survive its own aggression, perhaps it will be there, where our long-ago ancestors took their first steps.

Sleep is a dangerous time. It makes you vulnerable physically and mentally. I experimented with more wordy forms but decided that a short, punchy haiku was best.

184

"Sleep-waker" copyright © 1997 by Danith McPherson

This story first appeared in *The Fractal*, Summer 1997.

Although it is a continuation of Elizabeth/Elisbet's adventure in "Roar at the Heart of the World," it was published as a stand-alone story. I realized I could not let go of Elizabeth until she discovered important information about her own origin. So I wrote her out of childhood and into the next phase of her life. (Notice the title is waker, as in being awake, and not walker).

Meet the Author

DANITH McPHERSON lives in Minnesota. Snowy landscapes that sometimes show up in her stories are drawn from personal experience. She is often distracted from her writing by snowshoeing, kayaking, water skiing, astronomy, and scaring deer away from the bird feeder. In keeping with her Scottish heritage, she is a kilt maker and proudly wears McPherson tartan, especially at science fiction and fantasy conventions.

Website: www.danithmcpherson.com
FaceBook: Danith McPherson

9 781950 506002